In 1666, bribed with the King's Dowry—an ox and a cow, two pigs, a pair of chickens, two barrels of salted meat and eleven crowns in money—Yvette journeys from her native France to find herself a husband in the New World. But how will she choose the right man from all the eager settlers who await her arrival in Montreal? Fate takes a hand when she breaks her leg, for Captain Alain Renaud refuses to allow her to participate in the ceremony of the Choosing. 'You'll never be an old maid,' he reassures her. But Yvette wants to choose her *own* husband—and she will certainly not choose the arrogant Captain!

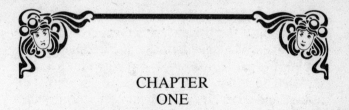

CHAPTER
ONE

'TODAY it begins,' Yvette told herself as she leaned against the rail of *Le Poisson Bleu*. 'The Choosing takes place when we land.'

She looked at the other girls gathered on the deck. Pauline wore red and white gingham, her black hair a gleaming coronet around her handsome face, her earrings with their red stones swinging as she spoke to Liliane, pretty blonde Liliane with her hair in two shiny braids with two little twisty curls in front of her ears. Liliane was wearing blue the colour of her eyes and she had a greenish blue kerchief on her head.

Yvette wondered if the others were as nervous as she was. All of them were laughing and talking. She heard little Marie-Rose beside her saying she hadn't slept a wink all night because she was so excited about landing in Québec.

All forty of the girls lined on the deck had been there for at least an hour watching in the early morning August sunshine of that important day in 1666 for their first glimpse of this new world. They had strained first to see the land, smoke trailing in the air from tiny chimneys, then suddenly the port itself with high cliffs and buildings nestled at their feet.

All aboard the bride ship had cheered, sailors, girls—even Madame Brioche the chaperon had wiped away a tear as they leaned over the rails huddled together, able slowly to distinguish tall houses and short houses, blue houses and grey and red.

It was as though *Le Poisson Bleu* was stationary and the town approached, becoming larger and larger as the minutes passed. Then the ship had berthed and the sailors with their huge ropes were tying her to the bollards.

Yvette let out her breath in a long sigh and patted her hair. Her dark brown hair fell naturally into soft curls at neck and forehead and into fat ringlets at the back. She was wearing her dark brown skirt and a coffee-coloured blouse and she knew they suited her. Her only ornament was a string of amber beads which had been her mother's and which brought out the amber brown of her eyes.

Some of the girls had their few belongings wrapped in shawls and carried them over their shoulders, clutching their few possessions to them for safety. Yvette thought with satisfaction of her own small trussing chest under the bench just away from the rail. She had two dresses in that, one a lovely dark green wool which she had made herself only last year under her mother's direction, two petticoats which she had bordered in lace, good leather boots and a plain cotton frock now a faded pink—it had been wine but she had worn it almost constantly on the voyage. She was lucky to have that much saved from that other life where the future had last year had so much hope.

The girls suddenly moved away a little towards the gangplank which was being lashed into position and, in her excitement, Yvette dropped her crutches.

Marie-Rose picked them up and helped her to the bench where her trussing chest was. She tucked the crutches in behind her and said, 'You sit here and wait, I'll tell you when we can go. You might as well be comfortable.'

Marie-Rose, small and dainty in her grey cotton with the pink bow Yvette had given her, her light brown hair gathered in a chignon down her back, went to join the others.

It was kind of her, Yvette reflected, and she could see everything from here. She could see people walking on the quay, a horse and cart, some soldiers marching up and down. Now why should they be there? Behind them she could see some sort of fortifications, and high up on top of the cliffs more walls and a rampart. Of course, there were battles with the Indians here and this town of Québec had to be defended against them. With the river at its front and those protective cliffs enfolding the houses on three sides, even to her untrained eye it seemed an easy place to defend.

The girls were not being allowed near the gangplank and Yvette wondered about that, for unloading appeared to have started.

More soldiers marched to the quay and there was a band with them playing a military air. Yvette watched them with pleasure. They made a fine show in their blue coats piped with white, their plumed hats, their muskets slung on their backs, their fine leather boots. Certainly they were smarter looking than any of the civilians.

The drums beat, the brass instruments shrilled and Yvette's senses stirred to their rhythm. The sun shone on her, the brightness of it mirrored in the water. She drank in the smell of the land, of damp earth and growing things, the breadth of the river, the noise and activity of the quay. This was Québec where she would find a home—and a husband, unknown, unnamed. She knew he was there: dark or fair, tall or short, handsome or ugly. None of that had seemed to matter all through the long nine weeks of the sea crossing.

But now the seeds of doubt were jostling in her mind. Would he be truly waiting and how would she recognise him as the right, the only, man for her?

Now Yvette began to fear the Choosing, which had seemed high adventure before. It would be the same for all the girls, she told herself. Were they feeling the same agony of uncertainty? She looked at them. Some faces were flat and expressionless, some were animated as they chattered to each other, but nowhere could she discover traces of the fear which racked her.

They had all listened carefully to Madame

Brioche, the chaperon, last night as she had explained the Choosing to them.

'You will all go together to one of the big church halls,' she had told them, 'and the men will be waiting there—just as eagerly as you. There will be at least five or six to every girl so it rests with you to choose well.'

'I want a handsome man,' Liliane had declared. 'I haven't come all the way from France to New France to marry an ugly fellow.'

Madame Brioche had clicked her tongue at that. 'The King's Dowry is not meant to buy beauty—but a good life for you. Think about the things that matter in a man: steadiness, a good worker, and a good provider.'

Liliane had protested that that was dull. She wanted excitement and some pleasure in life.

Madame Brioche had been disapproving. 'No one can put wise heads on young shoulders I suppose, but I beg you to think carefully. *Soyez prudentes, mes amies*.'

If Liliane was determined on her own way, Yvette was sure Pauline would make a very shrewd choice. And as to herself—she must do her best. She sighed and noticed that one of the army officers was coming on board, and behind him a well-dressed man, a fashionably dressed young man. They both stopped to speak to Madame Brioche at the head of the girls.

They drew her to one side so that she was nearer the seated girl.

'Are you in charge of these girls?' she heard the army officer ask in a deep, pleasant voice. He was a good-looking man with fair hair, a tanned face and dark eyes and held himself with a great deal of authority. The other man, dark and distinguished, was silent.

Madame was clearly disagreeing with him, but he was calm in the face of her gesticulating arms and loud protests.

'No, no, it was never arranged so,' Yvette heard Madame say. 'I must go with the girls to the hall.'

Then they began to speak with lowered voices so that Yvette could distinguish nothing of the conversation.

Customs men now came up the gangplank and engaged the ship's master in talk. He led them to his cabin and the army officer followed them.

Yvette took a deep breath and the tantalising odour of fresh bread baking came to her. What would she not give for a loaf of bread straight from the oven with butter to spread on it and a glass of milk to wash it down? Hard biscuits and brackish water had been the daily fare for weeks. Perhaps tonight she would dine on fresh food in her new home.

She shivered. Even with the hot sun on her shoulders she was suddenly cold. She did not want to face the Choosing. In fact, she did not want to marry at all, not this way, not instant marriage to a stranger. For how could he be anything but a stranger, this man who waited to wed and bed her by nightfall. She licked dry lips. There was no turning back.

Madame Brioche and the second man had come a little forward and seemed to be studying the girls, for Yvette saw him point to several of them in an unobtrusive way. He indicated Pauline and Liliane and Marie-Rose and herself and Madame must have supplied their names for he wrote something in a little notebook he carried. Then he followed the army officer to the master's cabin.

Yvette wondered vaguely what it was all about, but her attention was drawn to a party of dignitaries arriving by the side of the ship. It must be the mayor and his wife come to welcome the girls. Surely they would disembark soon.

Madame Brioche was waving to a florid-looking older gentleman who had arrived with a horse and buggy. It could be her husband. Now she had begun to marshal the girls. Some of them were trying to go down the gangplank and Madame was telling them that they must wait a little. Liliane and Pauline and Marie-Rose seemed to be in this number, and Madame signalled to her that she too must be patient, so Yvette settled back on her bench. Perhaps they were meant for a different hall. At any rate, the mayor was making a speech to the party of girls now assembled on the quay.

Yvette envied them the feel of solid ground under their feet.

Liliane came to join her. 'Madame says we must wait our turn,' Liliane's pretty face wore a frown of displeasure. 'She won't say when we may go. Why are they allowed on shore and not us? The men will see them first and not know there are more of us.'

Yvette tried to tell her there must be enough men to go round and secretly she couldn't help but be relieved at the thought of the Choosing not being immediate.

The girls who had left the ship were now being led into town. Two by two without a backward glance at *Le Poisson Bleu*, bundles in their hands or little trunks on their shoulders, they went. The shabby little procession followed the mayor and several little boys followed them. Yvette watched their progress up the hill.

Madame Brioche came over to Yvette and drew the remaining girls with her.

'I have news for you,' she exclaimed as the work of unloading went on all about them. 'You girls have been chosen to go on to Ville-Marie de Montréal to become settlers' brides there.'

'Ville-Marie de Montréal?' echoed Yvette. 'Where is that?'

'Only a hundred miles or so up the river,' replied Madame. '*Le Poisson Bleu* should convey you there some time tomorrow.'

'Tomorrow? Stay on the boat another day and a night?' There was a chorus of protests.

'Do you go with us, Madame?' Liliane asked.

Madame Brioche shook her head. 'No, no, my home is here in Québec. My husband waits on the quay. I understand there is a Madame Charette who will travel on the ship to Ville-Marie. She will be here presently.'

'But why?' the girls demanded. 'Why have the others been allowed to stay when we must go? It's not fair.' Their voices rose louder and shriller.

Madame did her best but to no avail. The more the girls thought about it and talked about it, the more upset they became. One or two threatened to run down the gangplank after the others. Liliane was hysterical, Pauline stamped her foot in rage and Yvette surprised herself by bursting into tears.

Madame slapped Liliane, and the sobbing girl began to run along the deck. The others followed to catch her.

Yvette looked up to find she was being watched. She blew her nose and knew her face was still tear-streaked.

'Go away,' she exclaimed crossly to the man who had arranged himself very comfortably on two new cargo-boxes opposite her.

'The waterfall's stopped, has it?' a very pleasant voice asked.

Yvette raised her eyes again and looked into laughing blue eyes in a handsome face. 'Yes'—her reply was stiff.

The man crossed one leg over the other. 'I think I'll stay. It's nice to talk to a pretty girl. What were you crying about?'

'The Choosing.' A last tear slid down Yvette's cheek.

'You're one of the little brides.' Her questioner

arranged a lace ruffle at his wrist. 'There's nothing to be nervous about. You'll be chosen.'

'That's just it,' Yvette retorted hotly. 'I won't. We've been told we have to go on to Ville-Marie de Montréal, wherever that may be—just the ten of us.' She pointed to the girls still surrounding Madame Brioche. 'And it was you who picked us. I saw you.'

'At least you cried quietly,' the man observed. 'That one's had hysterics.'

'That's Liliane.' Yvette was beginning to feel better. 'She gets excited.'

'And that flashy black-haired one stamped her foot,' he went on.

'Pauline,' Yvette supplied. 'Pauline is rather fiery.'

An amused blue eye winked at Yvette. 'Let me introduce myself. I am Marc Barbier and I am going on to Montréal where there are many men.'

'Yvette Deslauriers'—the girl could not be shy with this interested gentleman. What difference if they had not met properly?

The same idea must have been in his mind. 'You can claim me for an old friend,' Marc advised, 'otherwise when your chaperon is less busy she may want to chase me away—and that would be a pity, wouldn't it?'

Yvette nodded, mesmerised by his openness and friendliness. 'Where did we meet?' She fell into the deception.

'In France, of course,' he prompted, 'our families are old friends, cousins almost.'

He was, after all, Yvette reflected, very good looking and his jacket was well cut and of good material. The lace at neck and wrist was fine quality too. Her dressmaker's eye registered these details while her woman's eye approved the easy way he held himself and the pleasing shape of chin and nose. His forehead was high, his teeth white and his hair brown and wavy—but it was the eyes that held her, so blue, so well fringed with dark lashes, so alive.

'I used to visit where you lived,' he prompted. 'Where was it now?'

'At Sainte-Agathe, near Lyons,' a dimple showed in Yvette's cheek.

'Naturally, Sainte-Agathe—it all comes back to me. Your father was notary there.'

'No, no, my father's been dead for years. My mother was a dressmaker,' Yvette corrected. 'I lived there all my life.'

'Till now,' his tone was gentle. 'Now you'll live in Montréal, as I do.'

'This Montréal—what's it like?' Yvette enquired. 'Shall I like it?'

'Why not?' Another masculine voice broke in.

Yvette twisted round to see the speaker. It was the army officer who had first come up the gangplank with their orders to stay, and he was standing behind her. She had not heard him come. Seen close to, he was at once more and yet less impressive. He was not as tall as Yvette had thought, and rather broader in the shoulders and the chest. His eyes were brown and appraising, his hair straight and thick and fair where it showed under his soldier's hat. His face was browned by sun and wind. Where Marc's expression was bright and enquiring, this man's was stern, his chin firm, his mouth unsmiling.

'I heard a different story, Alain,' Marc waved a lazy hand, 'when you were posted to Ville-Marie.'

'Soldiers are not always pleased by their orders,' he retorted sharply, 'nor do they always enjoy passing them on.' His gaze rested on Yvette.

'Come, come, Alain,' Marc admonished him. 'Perhaps the fair Hélène did not want to see you go. Never mind, once the young ladies here have got used to the idea that this is not journey's end, you may enjoy escorting them—and your cannons—up the river.'

'*Peut-être,*' was the only reply. Yvette wondered whether that maybe referred to the fair Hélène or the girls on the boat.

'Are you to be in charge of us?' she asked him.

'Yes, Mademoiselle, and of twenty soldiers as well.' He tapped his foot impatiently against the deck. 'I could have done without the little brides.'

Yvette stiffened at the note of exasperation in his voice. 'If you are in charge, why did Marc pick us?' she queried.

'Soldiers delegate duties,' he replied stiffly. 'Anyway what does it matter? We sail within the hour.' He turned to Marc. 'Use that smooth tongue of yours to win these girls around. There are complications enough without unwilling passengers.'

The tone of his voice would have made Yvette angry if he had been talking to her, but Marc took it in good part. He winked at the girl as the officer left them and he beckoned to Madame Brioche to bring the girls nearer.

'Little Brides,' he addressed them. 'Do not be angry. I came especially to Québec to pick you girls for the settlers of Ville-Marie.'

'You did?' Pauline was standing beside him. 'Why us?'

'Because you're so pretty,' he declared, smiling at all of them. 'The good citizens of Ville-Marie de Montréal have been complaining that all the best girls are snapped up in Québec before our colonists have a chance to meet them—and the men of Montréal are very partial to beautiful women.'

A sigh went round the circle of girls. One or two smiled a little uncertainly.

Liliane laughed in delight. 'Why didn't you say so at first,' she demanded, 'instead of making us feel unwanted?'

He bowed to her. 'How could I say so before the others, Mademoiselle? It would have been too unkind.'

The girls looked at each other. Put like that, the whole situation appeared different.

'Why not take your bundles and boxes back to your cabins?' he suggested. 'If you leave them here they may be taken away with the cargo or stored as ammunition for the cannon.' He pointed lazily to two big guns which were being lifted aboard.

The girls began to giggle, whether at hearing their cramped sleeping quarters being referred to as cabins or at the thought of stockings or petticoats being stuffed into the cannons, Yvette wasn't sure. In twos and threes they left the bustling deck. There was no sense in losing their few possessions. Besides they would be able to spread themselves about, down below. They might even find an airier bunk, one nearer a porthole.

Liliane came and picked up Yvette's trussing chest. 'I'll bring it down for you,' she offered.

'Thank you.' Yvette was used to Liliane's help but she was pleased that it was given so willingly. She saw Marc smiling at her as the other girl took the chest.

'I know you are a superior sort of girl,' he observed, 'for the others wait on you—is there anything I can do for you? Something perhaps that you wish for?'

'As a matter of fact there is,' Yvette confessed, her eyes sparkling with mischief. 'Some fresh bread with butter melting on it.'

Marc laughed. 'That's easily granted.'

'Is it?' asked Yvette. 'Can we go to the bakery and choose some now?'

He shook his head regretfully. 'I think our good Captain Alain Renaud would have my head for that.'

Yvette looked at him sadly. 'Does he frighten you too?'

'At times,' Marc admitted. 'He's a marvellous fighting man—he was decorated twice in the campaign against the Indians last year. Captain Renaud shall provide you with fresh bread. I know he's bringing some on board for his men. There's no reason why he shouldn't share it with you girls. I'll go and speak to his corporal in charge of provisions.' He rose to his feet and left her.

Yvette stayed where she was. She liked it better up here in the fresh air and the sunshine and there was no point in unpacking if tomorrow would see journey's end again.

Captain Renaud was back now superintending the lashing and securing of his guns to supports on deck, and she watched him giving orders to his men. They seemed to take them willingly enough and one of them even made a suggestion and was clapped on the shoulder by the Captain for quick thinking.

Perhaps, the watching girl thought, in his own way and at his own job he might be excellent. He certainly had an air of command and confidence.

When a fat little woman in dark green came up the gangplank and waved to him, he broke off from his work and approached her. Within a few minutes he had brought the woman to the seated girl.

'This is Madame Charette,' he introduced her. 'She will chaperon you girls to Ville-Marie.'

Yvette smiled at her and she sat down on the

bench beside her. She had a fresh open face and a pleasant expression in her dark eyes. 'Tell me the names of the girls and what they are like,' she began, 'so that I may know them all and make them feel at home.'

Yvette warmed to her immediately. 'Of course,' she agreed.

'Where is Madame Brioche?' demanded Captain Renaud. 'Perhaps you would fetch her first.'

Before Yvette had a chance to rise, Madame Brioche appeared up the steps.

'Never mind,' the officer added. 'She is here. I shall escort her off the ship and then we shall sail.' He strode towards the chaperon and Yvette could only wave as she went to join her husband.

Yvette found Madame Charette very easy to talk to and she scarcely noticed as the gangplank was taken up and with the ropes loosened and the sails raised, *Le Poisson Bleu* left her anchorage and the town of Québec receded in the distance.

When they were under way Madame Charette suggested that Yvette should show her where she would sleep that night and the girl struggled to find her crutches which had by now become thoroughly wedged behind the bench. She rose to her feet and began to hop away talking to Madame all the while.

She was halted by a shout. 'Girl, stop where you are. I want to talk to you.'

Yvette froze while she heard Madame Charette gently tut-tutting.

Captain Renaud stood before her. 'Why are you on crutches?' he asked, frowning at her.

'Because I need them to get around.'

'I can see that,' snapped the Captain. 'Why was I not told about this?'

'I didn't know it mattered to you,' gulped Yvette, wishing she could get away from this inquisition.

'What were they thinking of in France,' the Captain fumed, 'to send a crippled girl to be a bride? Settlers need strong, able wives.'

That infuriated Yvette. 'I *am* strong and able,' she declared. 'I broke my leg on board this ship when a cargo box came loose. It was an accident.'

'Sit down,' barked the Captain, leading her back to the bench she had only just left.

Madame Charette accompanied them. 'There is no need to frighten the girl, Alain,' she protested.

The officer might not have heard her words for all the attention he paid to them. 'Let me see your leg,' he instructed the trembling Yvette.

'No,' she objected.

'Spare me the innocent maiden stuff,' he told her. 'Put your leg up on the bench and pull up your skirt—or I shall do it for you.'

Yvette stared at him mutinously.

'Do as he says, child,' said Madame Charette. 'He will not harm you in any way—I am here.'

'Whether you are here or not,' interjected the officer, 'I should like to wring her neck. This may be a dangerous voyage and I am saddled with a broken-legged virgin. You are a virgin, I suppose?'

'Yes,' Yvette nodded, 'but I don't see why you speak to me like this.'

Suddenly he smiled at her and his whole face softened. 'Let's see how it's going on,' he suggested.

Yvette raised her skirt without a further word. 'The ship's master set it—Captain Rolland himself—he said he was the best bone-setter on this savage sea.'

The officer examined her leg, touching the flesh firmly as though his fingers stripped it away and somehow felt only bone. 'A good, clean piece of work,' was his verdict, 'but the skin is shrivelled-looking.' He twitched her skirt back into position. 'You'll walk again—but not for a while I think—another three or even four weeks. The splints are good and firm, the bone is healing.'

Yvette was relieved to hear this diagnosis but she wouldn't allow him to know that. Instead she asked in a small voice, 'Is there much danger from the Indians?'

'There is always danger from the Indians,' was the repressive reply.

'Oh come, Alain,' interrupted Madame Charette pleasantly, 'we have just signed a peace treaty with the Iroquois.'

'Yes, for what's it's worth,' he agreed.

'Do you not think they'll honour it?' Madame Charette frowned.

'They have a different way of looking at things,' Alain pointed out, 'and I have heard rumours even though we marched on their villages this spring. In any case, individual Indians don't feel bound by treaties. They wage war on their own. Yet some of their ideas and ideals are excellent,' he added almost to himself.

'Which ones?' asked Madame.

'They believe land belongs to no one man but rather to everyone. That's probably why they allowed us to settle here in the first place.' The Captain seemed to have forgotten all about Yvette's leg. 'But of course,' he went on, 'we French believe in land and possessions and we keep looking for more.'

'You paint too harsh a picture of us,' Madame Charette objected.

'Do I?' He pointed to Yvette. 'Look at this child here. What has she come for? A husband and a home. And what is she bribed with to make the journey? The King's Dowry—an ox and a cow, two pigs, a pair of chickens, even two barrels of salted meat and eleven crowns in money. Isn't that true, Mademoiselle?'

'Yes,' Yvette replied, resenting the fact that these things had made her come. 'But when you have nothing you want a home and food to eat and land to own.'

Captain Renaud's eyebrows rose: 'Out of the mouths of babes,' he exclaimed and shrugged. 'You see, hungry French men and women will fight for what they want and the Indians now fight for the land and for their way of life. They'll destroy us or we them. It's a battle to the death.' He was silent for a moment. 'What's your name, girl?' he asked abruptly.

'Yvette.'

'Off you go, Yvette. I'll think about what must be done with you. I wish we'd left you behind in Québec. You would be someone else's responsibility now.'

Yvette, too, wished he'd left her behind. She didn't like the ominous ring of what must be done about her. If she had gone ashore at Québec she'd be a married woman now with a home of her own and a dowry that contributed to it. She led Madame Charette away.

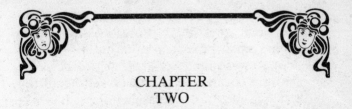

CHAPTER
TWO

LUNCH was a pleasant meal. The girls and their new chaperon gathered on the deck under the sails, and bread and butter, cheese and fruit were brought to them there. The soldiers ate on the front part of the deck and glanced often at the girls. Captain Alain Renaud and Marc Barbier shared the girls' portion of the deck.

The would-be brides devoted themselves to the food with enthusiasm and Alain told them they had the appetites of soldiers but Marc added they were a lot prettier. This made all of them giggle and it was a considerably happier party who sailed up the river towards Montréal.

The weather was sunny and very warm and they were glad of the breeze and the shade made by the sails. Their eyes were filled with the beautiful green of the trees and the bushes at the water's edge. Some of the girls, as the afternoon wore on, complained it was all the same: the unbroken forest, oppressive, secret, menacing, that they had seen since they had started up the St Lawrence River two days earlier.

Yvette loved the look of it with the dark green of

the fir trees and the contrasting lighter green of the others. Sometimes there were massive rocks, sometimes small protected bays, but everywhere she looked was grand yet satisfying to her. She smelled the cedars and the pines and heard the birds calling and the fish splashing, the sails creaking slightly in the wind, and the gentle thump of the river under the bows. She could not tire of it. She felt she belonged here. This new land was her home.

It became warmer and they sat about the deck, silent, almost asleep. Yvette began to think about that other life she had left for ever—France and her mother. She had blocked it out for so long but now, now, she could think of nothing else. Why had her mother taken Marcel Prudhomme as lover? Yvette had never understood why she had even liked him—and it had ended in disaster for her mother and for her. Monsieur Prudhomme had deserted her mother when she was expecting his child, and the dressmaking business which she had built up with such effort had melted away.

Her mother had been sure he would return, but he had not, so she seemed to give up; when the child was born dead she, too, had slipped away. Yvette had surprised herself by crying as much for the little half-brother who'd never drawn breath as for their mother. A poor tiny creature he had been, with hair like her own that curled about her fingers. She saw again that sad little face from her mother's coffin. They had been buried together, still lay together in the village churchyard, for the *curé* had been kind and had said that *le bon Dieu* forgave all, even though others had murmured and turned their faces against Yvette as though somehow she was to blame. It had been the *curé* too who had arranged for her to claim the King's Dowry and to come to this new world on the bride ship.

What neither Yvette nor the *curé* had foreseen was the presence of Pauline Cartier on *le Poisson Bleu*. Pauline was from the next village and had heard the gossip about Yvette's mother. She had mentioned it to Liliane and Liliane had mentioned it to someone else and they had all known. For a while Yvette had been shunned but after she had saved Liliane from the loosened cargo and broken her leg in doing so, the story had been forgotten. Perhaps in this new land there would be truly a new beginning. Perhaps too she could learn to have a little trust in men—they could not all be like Marcel Prudhomme.

Yvette sighed and stirred, aroused from her thoughts. *Le Poisson Bleu* no longer moved smartly along but floated slowly. It was even hotter and the wind died completely. The ship seemed to be motionless.

Yvette's leg was itchy and uncomfortable. She scratched at it then hopped about trying to ease it, going from one knot of girls to another, all of them upset and miserable.

Alain Renaud saw her and came towards her. 'It's healing,' he said. 'Put cold water on it and sit down before you have sunstroke.' He directed one of the soldiers to fetch a bucket of water.

Liliane found a cloth and helped her to bathe her leg. They were both so occupied with this task that they were startled when Marie-Rose cried, 'Indians, look, they're coming towards us! What shall we do?'

Liliane abandoned the water treatment and ran to Marie-Rose. All the girls were at the rail and Yvette could see nothing. She waited helplessly. Why weren't the soldiers doing something if this was an attack? She hopped to the rail.

A small boatload of Indians was paddling towards them. Fearfully she gazed at them. Naked, save for a loincloth of some kind of leather, their bronze bodies gleamed in the sunshine. Fierce in their bold movements, their canoe skimmed the water as fast as *Le Poisson Bleu* when the sails were full.

Some of the savages wore feathers in their hair—dark hair which was worn in a strange style—drawn back from their faces in a single thick plait to the middle of their heads. None of them had any hair at all on their faces.

The canoe halted at the ship's side and one of the Indians called out, 'We come in peace to talk with you.'

Alain and Captain Rolland held a hasty consultation and the master agreed to let the Indians on to the ship. He ordered a rope ladder to be let down over the side, and the men from the canoe swarmed up it. One by one they came, lithely, gracefully, effortlessly, and the girls fell back from the rails, but not before Yvette had noticed a second canoe with five or six more setting off from shore.

Seen close to, the natives looked even more menacing, for some of them had daubed their faces and chests with streaks of red and orange dye. One of their number spoke passable French and addressed a torrent of words to Alain Renaud calling him 'The Great White Father's Sword'. He asked to see the cannon and moved forward confidently to where the two guns stood. The others followed.

As they did so, the girls retreated.

'Why do you bring these weapons of death? Are your friends no longer your friends?' the speaker went on.

Alain did not seem perturbed by his questions or by the scowls of the others. 'Our friends are our good friends always,' he replied blandly. 'Have we not welcomed you here?'

A grunt was the only answer to this, and the questioner looked towards one of the others in the party, an older man than himself with three feathers in his knot of hair, and his hand on one of the cannon. This man spoke to the first in a very guttural language and at some length, while they all stood waiting for him. He looked a man of authority for all his nakedness.

Yvette found Marc was standing beside her and he nodded his head. 'Do you understand?' she whispered.

Marc nodded. 'So does Alain. That one's the chief and he wants to trade—to prove his good faith.'

That was the last thing Yvette would have expected. 'Trade what?'

'Sh-h-h,' Marc whispered back, 'furs, leather, you'll soon see. The second canoe will have the goods.'

This proved to be the case, although the interpreter spent a good deal of time establishing this and referring to the assembled girls as 'Alain's wives'.

Alain looked thunderstruck at this and the girls giggled uncontrollably though Madame Charette did her best to silence them.

When the second canoe came alongside, the first item passed up was a string of fish. 'Tempted from the river' was the way they were described—and indeed they looked fresh and appetising.

The fish were not bartered but presented to Alain, and he accepted them with a flowery speech praising the skill of the fishermen.

As a second present, a straw bag of small blue berries was presented to the 'wives' from the women of the tribe.

Yvette was then startled to be singled out for attention. The interpreter came to her with a small pottery jar and told her she should rub the substance it contained on her broken leg.

She thanked him and as he moved away she sniffed at the gift. The odour was overpowering.

'Bear grease,' Marc winked at her. 'Keep smiling. You don't want to offend them.'

Yvette kept the smile pinned to her face, mentally vowing that she'd never put that stuff on her leg and risk smelling like that.

Then the Indians produced leather slippers they called moccasins and several of the sailors bought these, using knives or combs or mirrors as money.

Once again the interpreter approached Yvette. This time with a pair of beaded moccasins. She fingered the soft leather, then shook her head regretfully. She had nothing to offer in exchange. She tried to explain and Marc told her she could use the beads she was wearing.

'They were a gift from my mother.' Yvette loved those beads. 'Besides, how would I manage to wear moccasins now? Look, I've had to make a hole in my slippers to fit the splints. No, no, I'll wait for another time.'

The Indian looked regretfully at her beads as she handed him back the moccasins.

Furs were now handed up the ladder and Captain Rolland picked out several skins and agreed a price. The mate too made a few choices of fox and lynx and several of the sailors picked small skins and paid for them.

'They'll make muffs or hats,' Marc told her and then went to examine some new skins that had appeared.

Once more, the interpreter approached Yvette. This time he held up three or four largish skins and allowed the girl to finger them. She marvelled at their softness, stroking the fur with a reverent hand. 'Beautiful,' she sighed.

'Beaver,' the salesman told her and his hand reached out to touch her beads.

Alain must have seen that hand, for he was immediately by her side.

'Good bargain, Mighty Sword.' As the interpreter stepped back, he was as aware of the warning look in Alain's eye as Yvette was. 'All four skins for your wife's beads.' He spread the skins on one of the cargo boxes.

'Do you want them?' asked Alain.

Yvette nodded. 'They'd make a lovely cape or a short jacket. Will he really trade them for my beads? Is that fair?'

'To him or you?' Marc drawled, joining them.

It was to Alain that Yvette looked for a decision.

'Beads are money to them,' he told her. 'They're good quality skins. If you want them, have them.'

Still Yvette hesitated. Her mother's beads were perhaps too big a price to pay.

'The furs will keep you warm in the winter,' Alain pointed out.

'A tailor won't charge much to make you something really smart,' Marc assured her, 'and with your colouring you couldn't do better than beaver.' His voice was caressing, mesmerising.

The interpreter looked at her and added a small lynx skin to the four beaver ones and sketched a hat.

Yvette's hand reached out to take the beads from her neck. She would remember her mother, beads or no, but the look of admiration in Marc's eyes was the kind of look any girl would sacrifice to keep.

The bargain was made and Yvette clasped her furs to her, half sure, half frightened, telling herself she'd need the warmth of them in the cruel cold of winter.

'Well done,' exclaimed Marc. 'I like a girl who's shrewd enough to act on a bargain. You won't be sorry. Sentiment weakens most women.'

Alain moved away, saying nothing, and Yvette looked at his retreating back. Had she expected him to say anything? It was nothing to do with him really and yet she felt a stab of disappointment. He might have given her a smile; funny, he hadn't even seemed to notice when the interpreter had called her his wife. Still she had felt protected and safe when he had moved so quickly to her side.

The Indians left shortly afterwards, but their coming had served to draw everyone together. Soldiers stood with sailors examining their purchases and offering their opinion as to quality. Not many of the soldiers had bought, but Yvette supposed this was because they had more opportunities to do so. Certainly they were acting as though they were experts at judging furs.

Captain Rolland came over to look at Yvette's skins and to display his. He laughed when he smelt the bear grease and pooh-poohed the idea of its efficacy.

Alain claimed his attention and the two men walked off together, deep in discussion.

It was still very humid and airless but by now the sun had lost a good deal of its heat. Alain came back and spoke to Madame Charette.

She called the girls to her. 'The Captains have decided we shall all share the fish for our evening meal and eat together on the deck.' She gave no explanation for this. 'We want to hold a concert after our meal. Now which of you girls can sing or dance?'

Pauline can dance,' Liliane volunteered.

'And so can Liliane,' Pauline declared. 'We'll dance together.'

Marie-Rose offered to recite and Yvette to sing, and three or four of the others said they'd sing in a group. So it was quickly arranged.

By the time the meal was ready they had all decided what they'd do. The sun was lower, and beautiful shades of red and violet and pink were vibrant in the sky and reflected back in the water. It was living colour, brilliant, awe-inspiring in its abandon and intensity. The river here was still very wide and lined with forests and a few big rocks, dark and threatening in this wild light.

Were savage Indians lurking behind them ready to attack now they had seen the size of the boat and the number of its crew? Yvette shivered at the thought. Perhaps that was why they were all going to stay on deck, alert and showing their presence.

In spite of these misgivings, Yvette enjoyed the

evening. The fish, boiled in the galley and served on deck, were delicious and accompanied by corn on the cob and tomatoes and bread, followed by apples and the berries the Indian women had picked, and then there were sweet cakes. Wine followed for Alain and Marc, and water mixed with wine for the girls.

It was a companionable meal with soldiers and the sailors not on duty mingling with the girls, but Yvette noticed that there were both soldiers and sailors on lookout duty. Marc exclaimed in a low voice so that only she could hear, 'Our Alain is an old fox. He's out to show the forest how relaxed we are, but not so relaxed as to be caught off guard. You can enjoy yourself. He knows what he's doing . . . and the moon will soon be up.' He looked up at the sky. 'A harvest moon tonight, big and full and red, and the sky will be full of stars later. What could be more romantic?'

Yvette inched away from him. There were times when the expression on his face reminded her of Marcel Prudhomme.

Marc's eyes still laughed as she did so but he put his hand on Pauline's arm and began to tease her about being a dancer.

Yvette felt restless and her leg had begun to itch again. She went over to the rail and faced the impenetrable forest, black now instead of green.

Alain found her there, rubbing her leg against the railings. 'Where's that bear grease?' he asked.

'I have it here.' She reached into the small bag she carried on a string attached to her crutches.

'Have you used it?' Alain was frowning.

Yvette shook her head. 'It smells.'

'Yes, it smells,' he agreed with her, 'but it's wonderful stuff. Use it.'

'Now?' Yvette knew he meant now. She recognised the voice of authority—whatever Captain Rolland might say in disparagement of the bear grease.

'Yes, now,' Alain replied, 'and don't turn those amber eyes on me. I mean to stand here and make sure you do—unless you'd rather I rubbed it on.'

'No-o,' Yvette responded in a small voice. 'That won't be necessary.' She sat down on the tail end of one of the cannon and began to knead the bear grease into her leg.

'It will stop your leg from shrinking,' said Alain beside her, shielding her from other eyes. 'I asked the Indians for it.'

Yvette shot a quick glance at him. 'Did you?'

He nodded. 'You should thank me for it.'

Yvette remained silent at that but her expression must have betrayed her feelings. Thank him for this evil-smelling concoction—never.

'There's no need to screw your face up in that silly way,' she was told. 'It only makes me realise that gratitude is not one of your virtues.'

Yvette's cheeks coloured up at this remark but it made her all the more determined not to thank him, not to say anything to him. Who was he to teach her manners?

'See if you can slide a little under the splints,' he advised her and she complied. 'Do that night and morning and I'll see about getting more for you when that's finished.'

'More?' stammered Yvette, her vow of silence forgotten. 'Am I to smell like this till my leg is healed?'

'You'll get used to it,' she was informed.

Yvette admitted to herself that the itching was becoming more bearable, but perhaps that was only because she found Alain's presence more irritating than her leg. She wished he would go away. The moon was rising, a great orange light, the harvest moon that Marc had foretold. She hitched her crutches under her arms and prepared to rise.

Alain Renaud put his hand on her shoulder for a moment. 'There's no need to move. You can answer a few questions for me.'

That fleeting physical contact jolted Yvette. Alain was like no other man she had ever met, not that she had met many men, she reflected—the curé, Marcel Prudhomme, the husbands of her mother's customers.

She rubbed her shoulder where he had touched it, wondering why it tingled so.

'What questions?' she enquired cautiously.

'Nothing difficult,' he assured her. 'Just satisfy my curiosity and tell me—what kind of man are you expecting for a husband?'

This was the last question she would have expected from Alain. 'I don't know,' she began shyly, trying to marshal her thoughts on a subject she and the other girls had talked about incessantly. She didn't want to discuss it with him.

'You don't know,' he snapped. 'You've crossed an ocean, Mademoiselle, to find a man and you still don't know what you want in him.' He leaned against the rail surveying her.

Yvette felt like a mouse captured by a predatory cat. Her eyes were fixed on his. She couldn't move, couldn't think. She licked dry lips.

'I can see you need a masterful man, one who'll decide for you.' The Captain shrugged. 'Let me give you a little advice.' He leaned down and picked up one of her hands and regarded it.

Again that strange prickling sensation attacked the hand he held and Yvette wanted to snatch it away from him, but she could not, though he held it loosely enough.

'Just as I thought,' he dropped her hand, 'not used to harsh work. Don't marry a farmer. Set your sights on a tradesman or a shopkeeper. That will suit you better.'

'Yes,' murmured Yvette, too bemused to offer more.

'Well at least you don't chatter on like some,' he observed, his eyes still holding hers. 'That can be very charming in a woman—if it means she has a quiet mind. Have you a quiet mind, or just an empty one?'

Yvette spluttered at that. For a moment words deserted her. 'You don't give me a chance to speak. You just talk yourself.'

He smiled at that, a frosty smile that didn't reach his eyes. Then he waited.

Silence stretched between them.

'Speak up,' he ordered. 'You complained I talked too much.'

Yvette was angry now, angry enough to forget that this man had power over her, might even dispose of her as he saw fit. 'Why should I talk to you?' she demanded. 'You think of me as a nuisance, another worry for you. You tell me what to do like you tell your soldiers; well, I'm not one of your soldiers. I don't want your orders.'

They glared at each other.

'If you were one of my soldiers you wouldn't raise your voice to me,' he observed silkily. 'But you're only a chit of a girl, a girl with more spirit than I thought. You'll need it here. Come, we must join the others. The concert begins.' He made no move to go, but waited for her.

Because with this last exchange he seemed more conciliatory, Yvette regretted her rudeness and wanted to make some amends. She searched for a safer topic.

'Do you mean to sing or dance?' she asked shyly.

For the first time his expression lightened. 'I shall sing,' he told her, 'a little love song about a girl with amber eyes like yours who scorns the man who loves her—until he marries another.'

That doesn't sound like much of a love song,' Yvette protested, not caring how he took that.

'Wait till you hear it before you make up your mind,' was his repressive answer. He strode away.

Yvette hopped after him, and the other girls made room for her on a bench. She was annoyed to find that Captain Renaud stood behind her.

The concert began with two of the sailors doing a dance over crossed sticks. This was followed by Pauline and Liliane who slapped their feet against the deck in time to an accordion accompaniment. Their dancing wasn't marvellous but they looked so pretty, one dark and one fair, and both so appealing. The audience demanded more.

Marc played the flute—a haunting little melody that kept them all silent and enthralled. He was excellent.

'Splendid,' Alain's voice broke in over the clapping. He leaned down to whisper, 'That will give the Indians something to think about. They hate our music.'

'He was good,' Yvette was indignant. Could Alain not even give proper praise where it was due? She ignored him, but she could not ignore the fact that he continued to stand there, just behind her, spoiling her enjoyment somehow.

Turn followed turn. There were acrobats and story-tellers interspersed with singers. Alain proved to have a pleasant baritone and his song was cheeky and cheerful. Marie-Rose recited a poem about a little girl who sickened and died. It was very moving.

Then it was Yvette's turn and she was half relieved, half annoyed, that the Captain had left the audience and gone to the rail to watch the further bank, or something on the river, perhaps.

Yvette's song was a lullaby, one her mother had often sung to her, and she sang it in remembrance, balancing herself on one crutch and rocking an imaginary cradle with the other. She saw Madame Charette wipe a tear from her eye, and some of the soldiers sighed. They all clapped and asked for more so she had them all join her in 'Frère Jacques'.

When she returned to her seat, Marc reached over and hugged her and exclaimed, 'What a splendid little mother you'll be.' Alain did not leave the rail.

The concert went on for a long time, the moon rising fuller and higher and the deep orangey light softening sky and water.

Yvette felt she was in a dream world as one of the soldiers played a soft homesick tune on his fiddle. She knew she should be tired. It had been a long exciting day but she wanted it to go on and on.

When the soldier began a sprightly number, everybody's feet began to tap and some stood up and danced.

Yvette longed to join them. It was then she was surprised to find Alain beside her again.

'A month or two from now,' he assured her, 'you'll be leading the dancing. What's a broken leg? It will heal.'

That cheered her a little. Perhaps he had a heart

after all. His next statement dispelled that thought quickly. 'When we reach Ville-Marie,' he announced, 'you won't go with the other girls.'

'Not go with the others?' Yvette echoed. 'Why not?'

'It wouldn't be right for a man to take a wife with her leg in splints. It wouldn't be fair.' Alain sat beside her on the now deserted bench.

'Not fair to whom?' demanded the indignant Yvette. 'Him or me?'

'To neither.' Clearly Alain was not going to enlarge on that. 'So you shall go to the hospital in Montréal and the good sisters will do everything to help you. Probably they won't put you to bed but they will make it easy for you till you are well and strong.'

If she had not been so bitterly disappointed or so tired, Yvette might have agreed with him but her temper got the better of her. 'What if I walk with a limp afterwards or my leg doesn't heal? I won't find a husband then. It will all be your fault if I'm an old maid and a servant all my days.'

Alain's lips twitched into a smile and then he laughed outright. 'There are scores of men in Ville-Marie de Montréal. You'll never be an old maid— not even if I have to find you a husband myself.' He put his hand on her arm but she jerked away from him. 'Just do as you're told and trust my judgment. I'm doing it for the best.'

How dared he? Yvette spluttered with rage. Who did he think he was to treat her this way?

The more she protested, the haughtier he became. 'The matter is settled,' he told her. 'You'll feel differently about it in the morning.'

He left her with that, and she watched the others dancing and having a good time. What did they care what she was suffering? What did anyone care?

Yvette was stunned and near to tears but it was too hot to go below. She no longer felt in a party spirit. It was all very well for the others. How she would have enjoyed dancing. No one even came to talk to her.

Thoroughly depressed, she eventually followed the others down, glad she did not have to share her cabin with any chaperon tonight, for Madame Charette had elected to share one of the larger rooms with the other girls. Yvette felt that the slightest kindness would have made her break down.

Once in bed, though she was very tired she could not sleep and tossed and turned, finding it unbearably hot. The ship was absolutely motionless and this was so unnatural after the weeks of sailing that it contributed to her sleeplessness. The moon shone in through the porthole so that a ghostly light fell on the other empty bed.

Yvette turned the Captain's words over and over in her mind. She was not to take part in the Choosing. Instead she must go to hospital until her leg was better. As she lay there she wondered if there was not something she could say or do to change that decision. Perhaps if she pleaded with him, smiled at him, kept her angry resentment under control, he might give way and let her go with the others after all.

If only she weren't so hot and uncomfortable and lonely, the magic words might come to her. If she could get a breath of air she'd feel better. Well, why not? The cabin door opened on to the passage and there was no one to see her if she crept up on deck. She knew it was forbidden ground at night but everything was different tonight.

She swung herself out of bed and slipped her skirt over her nightgown.

'Quietly, quietly,' she cautioned herself as she hopped over to the door and opened it gently. Balancing on her crutches she climbed the steps, glad the ship was motionless or she'd never have managed on her own.

A quick peep at the top assured her that there was no one at this end of the deck and she manoeuvred herself so that she could cling to the rail and slide along it soundlessly.

She had almost reached the bench where she had sat all morning when she was seized from behind in an iron grip and her crutches slid from her grasp to the deck.

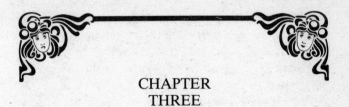

CHAPTER
THREE

'WHERE were you going and whom were you planning to meet?' It was Captain Renaud's voice. Yvette recognised it at once.

She was held prisoner against his firm body in spite of her struggles and protests.

'I knew it was you,' he groaned, 'because of the crutches. Why are you more trouble than all the rest of them put together?' He did not release his grip but only held her tighter. 'We'll leave your sticks where they fell. You can't move without them.'

'I can't move anyway,' gasped Yvette. 'You're hurting me.'

'I may hurt you more,' was the stern answer to that plea, 'when I find out whom you were expecting to meet here.' He shook her. 'Tell me—I'll find out anyway.' He turned her to face him.

'No one, let me go,' begged Yvette, breathless in his embrace, her heart beating such a tattoo against him that she was certain he must feel it.

The moon which had been half hidden behind a cloud emerged and bathed the deck in light. Captain Renaud's face was dark and threatening above the girl's. Abruptly, he released her, dumping her like an unwanted parcel on the bench by the rail.

'We'll wait, shall we,' he suggested, 'to see if he turns up?' He leaned against the rail so he could watch her and watch the deck.

'You'll wait a long time then,' Yvette told him, her voice still trembling with the shock of being his captive. She wondered where she found the courage to reply to him when every nerve in her body was screaming messages of warning. 'I'm not meeting anyone.' Her mouth would hardly open to utter that.

'I think you may be right,' Alain agreed pleasantly. 'It's likely he stole away when he heard us.' He sat beside her. 'You'll just have to make do with me, won't you?'

That had such an ominous ring about it that the girl tried to shrink away but the Captain pulled her to him. 'Wouldn't you say any girl who came up on deck half-dressed in the middle of the night was looking for something?' He fingered the lace at the neck of her nightgown. 'Something we all look for in the lonely darkness,' he added more softly. 'Well, I can provide that comfort as well as the next man.'

Yvette's head was held against his shoulder now and he was forcing her head back so that she had to meet his gaze.

She shuddered. 'No, please don't,' she begged as his meaning became clear to her. She was trembling with his hand on the bare column of her neck.

Terror touched her tongue. 'I—I couldn't sleep,' she gasped.

'Neither could I,' he whispered. His lips brushed hers, a butterfly above a flower.

She tried to slide along the bench, to escape from him. This must be happening to someone else, not her. She hadn't asked for his kiss or his embrace, didn't want either, but his lips fastened on hers.

They were rough, urgent, demanding; what they demanded she wasn't sure, but her body shook with feelings she didn't understand, couldn't control.

It was no use. She couldn't fight this man. She went limp in his grasp and would have slid to the deck except that he was holding her, forcing her to respond.

He raised his head at last, his arm still firmly round her waist. 'What if one of my men had found you—or one of the sailors—my foolish little virgin—do you suppose they would have treated you as gently as I have done?'

Gently? Yvette felt trapped and exhausted. She shrank away from him—as far as it was possible in the circle of his arm. A turmoil of conflicting emotions shook her. He had kissed her to teach her a lesson. That was what he was telling her. It hadn't been because he wanted her. Even in her inexperience she knew that. His kiss had burned and scalded her with that message. He might have taken a wanton that way. And he'd called her a foolish little virgin—his foolish little virgin. She was not his and vowed she never would be. Perhaps she'd stay a virgin if this was what all men were like.

Alain laughed. 'You didn't like it much, did you? It frightened you, that kiss; well, it was meant to. A girl who's fool enough to arrange to meet a man on deck needs a sharp lesson in the ways of men. I think you may have learned it.'

'You shouldn't have done it. I didn't come to meet anyone.' Yvette tried to gather some tattered remnants of dignity and self-respect around her. Her hair felt tumbled, her skirt was rumpled and creased. There was a piece of lace hanging by a thread from the bodice of her nightgown. She fingered it nervously, attempting to put it back in place, but to no avail. It must have caught on one of the buttons of his tunic when they struggled. What must he think of her to treat her so? She wanted to shout at him that he had no right to touch her, to rouse feelings in her which had been dormant . . . she put that thought out of her mind quickly . . . 'The *curé* says only married couples should kiss like that.'

That, instead of putting him in his place, earned a great shout of laughter.

'*Pauvre petite enfant*,' he was still chuckling as he released her. 'What does your *curé* know of marriage? He is celibate, like you.' He made that phrase 'like you' almost a sneer, as he rose to his feet and looked out on the river. Then he turned back to her. 'Do you suppose he knows the feelings between men and women that he so glibly talks about? Did you have any idea about them—before tonight?'

Yvette ignored that last question. She couldn't answer it truthfully, so better not to answer it at all.

'Of course the *curé* knows.' Her voice lacked the certainty she would have liked as her world rocked at the thought that Alain might be right. The *curé* was an old man. He'd lived a long time, she told herself, but perhaps there were things between men and women . . . she hadn't known what a kiss could be like. Her tongue inched its way around her bruised lips.

'Why did you really come on deck?' Alain didn't bother to argue about the *curé*'s knowledge.

'It was so hot down below,' Yvette stammered. 'I wanted to think.'

His eyebrows rose. 'So you wanted to think—if you had thought, you wouldn't be here.'

Yvette wondered how long Alain meant to keep her here. She couldn't move without her crutches. She was still his prisoner. She sighed. What did he mean to do with her? At least she felt safer now with him standing by the rail. What if he held her again? She would scream, of course that's what she'd do, what she should have done before. As it was, every time she opened her mouth with this man, she only made things worse for herself. He was just waiting to trap her, to make her more upset.

'Go on,' he prompted, 'what was it that required this deep consideration?'

'My future,' Yvette replied resentfully. 'I wondered . . .' she faltered, then went on with a rush, 'if I couldn't get you to change your mind about me going to hospital.' She looked down at her hands, clasped together like a suppliant's and despised herself for begging from this man.

He stood leaning against the rail facing her, the moonlight full on his face, sharpening the strong angle of his jaw. When he spoke it was quietly, almost to himself. 'Three Feathers, the Indian Chief who gave me the bear grease for you this afternoon, told me the only sensible thing I could do with you was load you with gifts and return you to the Sun King, the Great White Father over the sea who had sent you. A hoppity woman would be no use to me, he said. I wish I could take his advice.'

He sat down on the bench again, this time at the far end and his expression was no friendlier than his wounding words.

'A hoppity woman to be fobbed off with gifts'— Yvette could have cried with humiliation and rage. Couldn't Alain see that was exactly what she feared? She bit her lip as he went on.

'I don't know why he thought you were my woman, but he suggested I choose one of the others instead.' Alain shrugged. 'Since I am only a soldier I have no claim to any of you. You are brides for the settlers. In Three Feathers' village, warriors have the pick of the girls, and he rated you highly because of your bargaining ability—but enough of that—what have you to use to bargain with me?

You kiss like a child, a girl who hasn't been awakened yet. How old are you?'

'Seventeen,' she replied in a small voice, 'but some of the girls are younger than that. Marie-Rose is sixteen.'

'Seventeen,' he repeated musingly, 'not very old to have crossed an ocean to find a husband—was there none at home?'

'Not without a dowry,' Yvette whispered (and might have added, 'and with a disgraced mother'), but he was speaking again.

'You're hardly more than a child, determined to meet life head on. I've no doubt you'll find life here—and wish you could go back to childhood.' He reached over and patted her knee as if she had been five years old.

'I'm not a child,' Yvette protested.

'Yes, you are,' she was told firmly. 'Consider yourself lucky I'm giving you the chance to grow up a little before marriage is thrust upon you. One day you may become a woman, a woman who knows passion and desire— but not yet awhile. You're young and innocent. A man wants a woman you know, even a hoppity woman, but not a silly girl. Now off to bed with you. I'll get your crutches.' He rose to his feet.

Yvette felt as though he'd slapped her. She couldn't help being seventeen. 'You're horrible, I hate you,' she muttered under her breath, still too much in awe of him to say the words out loud.

If he heard them he made no sign, but only bent to retrieve her property, then straightened with a finger to the night. 'Do you hear it and feel it?' he asked. A breeze is blowing. We'll be in Ville-Marie tomorrow—today I mean.' He handed the girl her sticks. 'Get some sleep. I'll watch you down the stairs.'

Before she knew it, Yvette was back in her cabin, still smarting from that encounter. Captain Renaud thought she was a child, a child to be told to go to bed, to get some sleep—when he had banished sleep by his brutality and harsh words. He had got rid of her when it suited him, kissed her when it suited him. She hated him as much for that kiss as for his sharp dismissal of her womanliness.

Horrible, hateful, sneering man, he'd laughed at her as well. And his lips had assaulted hers unmercifully . . .

Liliane woke her in the late morning with a roll and a bowl of gruel. 'The sun's shining,' she told her, 'and we shall reach Ville-Marie this afternoon. We all slept in. Wasn't the party fun last night?'

By the time Yvette was up and dressed and had joined the others on the deck they were all still talking about the party. She felt she had left such childish things behind.

Lunch was another relaxed meal. One of the sailors had caught some eels and there were enough for all. The bread wasn't as fresh as it had been the day before but it was very palatable still.

Yvette looked about for Captain Renaud and hoped she wouldn't see him. Marc was very much in evidence and was friendly. Madame Charette had heard about her going to the hospital and had a little chat with her about it.

'It'll be much the best thing for you,' she told her. 'The hospital is called Hôtel-Dieu, God's hostel, and Jeanne Mance, who is in charge, is kindness itself and has been in Montréal since 1642 when it was founded. You'll like her. Alain is quite right. He'll see you get there while I go with the rest of the girls to the Choosing.'

It no longer seemed so terrible to Yvette to wait until her leg had healed completely. The thing that bothered her was how she would greet Captain Renaud or he her. Would he refer to last night? She felt very shy about facing him. She would be sure to blush or stammer and everyone would know that he had kissed her.

But as it happened they were all studying Ville-Marie from the ship's rail when he appeared, and he went immediately to speak to his soldiers. Yvette breathed a sigh of relief and watched the town coming into view.

Montréal seemed much less protected than Québec. True, there was a fort at water's level and a small mountain rising sharply from behind that, but many of the houses were outside the fort seemingly undefended except for small log redoubts. The houses themselves in straggling lines looked small, the roofs were peaked like witches' hats, the framework white with brightly-coloured doors. And now that she looked more closely she could distinguish that some of them had palisades of their own; for defence, she supposed. A thrill of fear stirred her. This island, surrounded by two rivers, must be in the front line of attacking Indians.

Yet it looked a bustling place with stores, trading-posts and warehouses.

'It is the fur trade that makes Ville-Marie so important,' Marc told her. 'You see it can not be bypassed by the canoes from the north and west bringing the skins to market. You will be surprised by the quality of the goods in the shops. In fact this ship will be carrying bales of rich materials for clothes, and fine furniture crated up as well, even crystal chandeliers and the best of wines. Not much was off-loaded in Québec.'

There were people waiting on the quay and a great cheer went up as *Le Poisson Bleu* docked. The girls waved and the men and women and children gathered there waved back.

This was a friendly place, Yvette reflected. They were all laughing and chattering to each other.

She noticed too that there were canoes on the river and at water's edge, and Indians on the quay, standing silently or walking among the townsfolk and no one seemed to mind.

The girls began to gather their possessions and to come in a circle around Madam Charette.

Marie-Rose came to Yvette and kissed her, saying, 'I shall come and see you when I can.'

Then Liliane turned to her and hugged her. 'I'll bring my new husband to visit you.'

'You'll find a husband too,' Pauline told her without much warmth in her voice.

Then the others clasped her hands and wished her well before Madame Charette led them away.

Yvette felt an enormous lump in her throat and tears forming in her eyes as they went.

'Good luck,' she called after them. '*Bonne chance*.' And she was torn with a desire to follow them. She hitched her crutches under her arm and felt Alain's hand on her shoulder as she tried to lift her little case.

'Not so fast,' he exclaimed. 'The hospital is some distance and there's no need for you to carry that.' He led the way down the gangplank while a soldier appeared at his signal and shouldered her little trussing chest.

The angle of the gangplank was a little awkward for the girl, but she was determined she wouldn't ask Alain for help. She managed to reach the quay a little out of breath, but triumphant.

'There's a horse and cart waiting,' Alain pointed to the vehicle, 'just a few steps away.'

She kept pace with him as he walked towards it.

The horse was tired-looking and the wagon just a flat farm-cart with slatted wooden sides reaching to a height of half a metre on two sides. Against these sides, several bags and boxes were stacked.

'It was all I could find.' The soldier came from beside the driver at the horse's head as his fellow deposited Yvette's trussing chest in the cart. 'There aren't any carriages.'

'It'll have to do.' Alain looked at it without any expression. He lifted Yvette up to join her trunk and handed her her crutches. She sat rather gingerly on the bare floor, which appeared to be clean.

'Cut along and join the others,' he instructed the two waiting soldiers.

Did he mean to give orders to the driver or perhaps join him on the front seat, the girl wondered, and was surprised when Alain swung himself up beside her in the back and signalled to the driver to start.

Encouraged by the crack of the whip, the horse moved off, the cart rattling behind her. Yvette hoped it wasn't far. It was already uncomfortable.

'I didn't know you meant to come with me,' she stammered.

Alain's eyebrows rose. 'It would not be kind to send you on your own in such a conveyance.'

Yvette tried to conceal her reaction. When had this man been kind to her?

The girl leaned back against one of the sacks and stretched out her legs. As the horse fell into a shambling trot she found herself swaying against her companion and she held on to one of the wooden slats at the side to balance herself. She meant to give the Captain no cause to criticise her conduct. After last night she didn't want to come in contact with him.

In silence, Alain did the same.

They left the quay and Yvette looked through the space between the slats and had her first close glimpse of Ville-Marie de Montréal. It was quite different from Québec. There, there had been sheer bare cliffs enclosing the harbour. Montréal was backed by a green mountain on the top of which stood a cross. It was from this hill that it took part of its name—Mount Royal.

On the flat level where the cart was proceeding now, Ville-Marie was a fort as much as a town. She could see that now that she was close to it. The streets though were tree-lined and provided shade against the fierce sun.

She didn't want to start a conversation with him but she must speak. 'I hadn't expected it to be so green,' Yvette murmured, excited to view it all, 'or there to be so much water.'

'It's because two rivers meet here,' Alain told her. 'The Indians come here to trade in their canoes for rivers are the highways here. They all come in the autumn when the fur fair is held. I'm afraid it is a time for the nervous to stay in their homes and pray.'

'Why?' asked the girl, curious and alarmed.

'Because the worst of the traders give the Indians brandy in exchange for furs,' he replied, 'and then there are fights and brawls. They are not used to strong drink.'

Yvette digested this information in silence. The horse had now begun to ascend a slope and its pace slowed and the clinging to the slats became more difficult. Yvette found herself sliding gently to the tail of the cart however much she tried to remain where she was.

'Hold on to me,' Alain advised. He put his arm about her waist.

Yvette hesitated and wanted to move away, but it would be foolish to risk her leg. She should have felt a lot safer, but she felt breathless and her pulses raced. She didn't like this officer, resented his interference in her life. Why was his nearness affecting her like this?

'I never thought to arrive this way in Ville-Marie,' she declared.

'Nor I,' he added dryly as they rolled against each other. 'You're trembling,' he exclaimed. 'There's no need to be frightened of staying in hospital.'

'No,' Yvette's breathing was uneven in this enclosed space with his body so close to hers that she could feel its warmth and strength. Why had he supposed it was the thought of hospital that had alarmed her? 'I won't have anyone to visit me,' she said, to take her mind off his presence.

'Nonsense,' Alain told her, tightening his grip on her waist, 'the girls will visit you. I heard them promise to.'

'If their husbands let them,' the words were jerked out of Yvette, due as much to the jolting of the cart as to the uncertainty of her situation.

'I always visit any of my men who find themselves in hospital,' Alain announced. 'I shall consider you as one of them and come to see how you go on.'

'Thank you,' murmured Yvette, not sure she wanted to be numbered as one of his men. At least that put things on an impersonal basis and she was grateful for his promise. Last night she had never wanted to see him again. It was different today. She might have no one else to turn to. It was good of him to offer.

It might indeed be different today—but not so different that she didn't realise she shouldn't be sitting here with his arm about her however well hidden they were by the sides of the wagon. Yvette bit her lip. How could she move?

The driver suddenly reined in his charger, and Yvette disentangled herself quickly. She warned herself to be careful. She wanted no repetition of last night. He did not care for her. An officer in the King's army could have no lasting interest in a penniless orphan girl who had only that same monarch's dowry to marry a settler. All of the girls had been warned often enough by Madame Brioche to stay clear of the sailors on *Le Poisson Bleu*. The same must apply to the soldiers, and above all to this one.

She reached behind her and drew a box forward from the collection in the cart and wedged one of her crutches between it and the side of the cart. That would serve as a bulwark.

Alain straightened himself and regarded the obstruction between them. 'Very wise,' he observed. 'You have a disturbing effect on a man.'

Yvette coloured. That was the first sign he had

given that he was human enough to acknowledge her presence had some effect on him. That pleased her though she wasn't sure that she wanted it. She shrank back further in the corner she had now made for herself. She didn't understand him. He had no pretty phrases, no flattery. Instead he was direct—and honest; she had to admit that. Surely they were good qualities. How did he manage to use them to upset her then?

She found nothing to say to him as the horse clip-clopped along the deserted street. He wasn't even looking at her, but seemed wrapped in his own thoughts. Perhaps he was regretting bringing her himself when he could have delegated the duty.

'Nearly there,' Alain announced as the cart moved forward again and he swung his legs over the tailboard and balanced there, having put a good deal of distance between himself and her.

The street came to an end with a large house set in some grounds, and here they stopped and Alain helped her down.

Yvette propped herself up on her crutches and Alain carried her trunk in at the front door. The cart went round to the back, presumably to enable some sort of delivery from the assorted sacks and boxes.

An old nun came to them as they hesitated in the hallway.

'Sister Jeanne,' cried Alain as the nun kissed him on both cheeks. 'How nice to see you—and looking so well.'

'And you, dear boy,' she stood back smiling. 'How's the arm?'

'As good as new,' he waved his left arm in the air.

Yvette looked at him. He hadn't mentioned anything about being in hospital or being wounded but she supposed that was a soldier's lot.

'And whom have we here?' Sister Jeanne turned her attention to the girl. 'I haven't seen you before.'

'No,' Yvette replied. 'I've just come. I should have been married today.' There was something so sympathetic about this woman that Yvette wanted to talk to her.

'You see that was impossible,' Alain explained. 'I have brought her to you, Sister Jeanne, till her leg is whole again.'

'You have done well,' the nun clearly agreed with him. 'We shall be happy to have her here with us—and perhaps she will find a husband without having the ordeal of the Choosing. You can safely leave her with me.' She put her arm on Yvette's shoulder. 'First I shall have a look at your leg and then we'll see what's best to be done. The good Captain can visit you tomorrow.'

'Yes, of course,' Alain agreed, and added, 'if my duties will permit.' He took his leave with a simple, '*Bonjour, Mademoiselle, bonjour, ma soeur*', and Yvette watched him go with more emotion than she expected. She hoped he would return to see her.

Yvette settled in to hospital life quite happily. The nuns were kind. Sister Jeanne had inspected her leg and then turned her over to a young fresh-faced sister with merry brown eyes, Sister Marie.

Sister Marie assigned her to a tiny cell of a room. It was plain white, bright and sunny, and the bed though narrow was comfortable. There was a table and chair and a cheery spread and curtains. A crucifix on the wall was the only ornament.

'I've put you in here,' she said, 'because there is no need for you to spend all your time in bed or to mope around. If you wish to help me in the mornings with the mothers and the babies I shall be very pleased with your company. In the afternoons when the heat is at its greatest you may rest on the veranda, which is cool. You'll soon get to know all the patients and will have company to talk to.'

And so it proved to be. It was only a small hospital with two main wards, one for men and one for women. There were also a few small rooms down the corridor for emergencies or delivering babies.

That evening Yvette met all the patients. As it happened, there were not many. A man and a boy shared the men's ward. The man had a head wound, the other a crushed leg. 'Both are soldiers,' Sister Marie told her.

Three young mothers were in the women's ward and one of them had twin boys. When Yvette admired them she won an immediate friend, and sat and chatted with her.

Before she knew it it was supper-time and the meal was surprisingly good. There was a nourishing

stew with lots of vegetables, fresh bread, and cus-
tard pie. It was followed by a hot drink Sister Marie
said was her own concoction—maple syrup plus a
touch of vinegar and hot water.

Candles and lamps had been lighted and the
babies given their last feed of the day when Sister
Jeanne asked Yvette to come to her office for a
moment.

'A new patient was admitted tonight,' she told
her, 'an old woman by the name of Madame Brun-
Cartier.'

'Do you wish me to give up my room?' asked
Yvette, wondering why she was being consulted.

'No, that will not be necessary,' Sister Jeanne
smiled. 'Madame Brun-Cartier will have that little
room just off the main ward, but I would like you to
talk to her, be a friend to her if you can find it in
your heart to do so.'

Yvette nodded. 'What is wrong with Madame?'
she asked.

Sister Jeanne shrugged. 'She complains of many
aches and pains but I think it is an illness of the soul.
She is lonely and needs young company and an
interest outside herself. You will not find her easy
perhaps but it would please me if you would try.'

'I shall do my best,' Yvette said. 'Has she any
family here?'

'Not now,' Sister Jeanne sighed, 'but I think I will
let her tell you about that in her own good time. I
thought at first of putting her in with the mothers
and babies but she might lose her sleep that way.'

Yvette was impressed with the consideration Sister Jeanne was devoting to this patient, and wondered if they were friends of long standing. She was also pleased to be asked to do something in return for her stay in the hospital.

She went to her bed that night, content to be in this place and wondering too how the other girls had fared.

In the morning she followed Sister Marie round at her duties and spent a good deal of time with the babies and the mothers. She brought Madame Brun-Cartier her breakfast and was greeted with the remark, 'What is it? Gruel? I never eat breakfast anyway.'

The old woman was very thin and gaunt-looking, big-boned and white-haired, dark-eyed with great circles under her eyes, and a fierce expression.

'Sister Jeanne will want you to eat,' said Yvette, smiling. 'It's very nice porridge and there's honey with the bread.'

'Leave it then,' said Madame Brun-Cartier, 'and hop away. I don't like being watched.'

Yvette did as she was told. She could see Madame was going to be hard work. And though she was in and out several times in the morning she never got more than a few ungracious words from her.

After a good lunch of home-made soup and potatoes and cold meat and gravy, Yvette was very glad to go out on the veranda and install herself in a comfortable wooden chair on the screened-in portion, with her needle and thread to mend a petticoat which her crutches had torn. When she finished that she would mend the lace on her nightgown.

Sister Marie brought out Madame Brun-Cartier to join her. 'Madame says she wants a little nap, but Sister Jeanne feels the fresh air will do her good,' she explained.

Madame said nothing.

Grass and trees in the grounds were hazy green and it was very warm. It was good to sit and rest. Soon the sewing slid from Yvette's hands and both she and Madame Brun-Cartier slept.

Yvette woke because something was tickling her nose. She tried to brush it away but it still tickled. She opened her eyes to find Marc Barbier bending over her with a long piece of grass in his hand.

'What a charming picture you make asleep in the sun,' he whispered. 'You're healthier-looking than your companion.' He picked up the petticoat and examined the lace of its edge. 'Your handiwork?'

Yvette nodded, 'Yes, I made the petticoat, now I'm repairing it.' She stretched out her hand to take it from him.

He easily held it out of her reach. 'Nice, even, stitches,' he observed and, admiring it, added, 'and very feminine. Tell me, have you the true dressmaker's eye for style and material?' He spread it out, surveying it. 'Yes, perhaps you have.' He relinquished the garment to her.

'Why do you want to know?' asked Yvette, not

quite sure that a gentleman should examine her petticoat—and so closely.

'I have an idea. I'll tell you about it afterwards, but first I've come to bring you the news. Aren't you wondering how your friends have fared?' He perched on the veranda rail and looked down at her.

'Oh yes,' breathed Yvette. 'I'd love to hear.'

'Pauline has landed on her feet,' he announced. 'She's married Pierre Michelin, a shopkeeper. Clever, handsome, young, with an eye for the ladies is Pierre. Yes, they'll deal famously together. Unless I miss my guess Pauline will use a firm hand with him.'

'And Liliane?' Yvette prompted. She might have known Pauline would do well. 'Did she find the handsome man she wanted?'

'Handsome, yes,' Marc conceded, 'but not the best husband-material, I would have thought.'

Yvette frowned. 'Why?' It upset her to think Liliane hadn't chosen wisely.

'He's a nearly man,' Marc shrugged. 'Nearly built a house—only the roof came off in a storm and he had to get someone else to finish it—nearly got a commission in the army only something happened at the last minute and it fell through—nearly made a fortune on furs last year only he lost half of them in the rapids—well it always seems to be like that for him.'

'He must be more than nearly married,' Yvette pointed out.

Marc laughed. 'Perhaps this will change his fortunes.'

'What about Marie-Rose?' Yvette hadn't forgotten the timid little girl who had been her first friend.

'The little dark one? Pauline said she'd found a good farmer. Most of the others did too. Think of it, you might have been a married woman today.' He teased her.

'Well, I'm not,' Yvette's voice was sharp. 'What was the idea you had about my petticoat?'

Marc didn't answer her directly. Instead he asked, 'Have you decided what you want made with those beaver skins?'

Yvette shot him a surprised glance. 'Yes, as a matter of fact, I have. I'd like a longish jacket, flared at the back and with pockets, I hope, but I've never worked with fur,' she finished uncertainly.

'Don't even think of it,' he advised. 'You need a furrier and I know just the man.'

'But I haven't any money,' objected Yvette, raising her voice a little.

Madame Brun-Cartier stirred but didn't open her eyes.

'Sh-h,' Marc laid a finger against his lips and winked at her, 'all in good time. The first step is to go to Pauline's husband's shop and have a look at the materials he has for sale. I want to know what you think of them for quality dresses.'

'And then?' Yvette waited for more. But more he would not tell her though she smiled and pleaded.

'How will I get to this shop?' She was impatient with him now. 'It'll be too far on crutches.'

'That's a little problem you'll have to solve for yourself,' he told her. 'But I never knew a woman whose curiosity has been aroused who couldn't overcome a few obstacles. Put your mind to it.'

Yvette could have hit him. Why was he being such a tease when she wanted to know what it was all about?

He only smiled and changed the subject. 'A word of warning—don't let Sister Marie talk you into doing the accounts, whatever you do.'

'Why not?' Yvette frowned, knowing she'd already half promised to do that very thing.

Marc laughed. 'She uses the religious system.'

Yvette was puzzled. 'I've never heard of that.'

'I suppose any other system would drive her mad,' Marc admitted. 'The hospital doesn't really have an income. It exists on charity and donations. Sister Jeanne has raised some money in France, and the army manages to spare flour and sugar in odd handouts. Some of the men in the outside community bring in a deer or some fish and now and again when a farmer kills a pig he sends sausages or bacon—well you can imagine what that does to the bookkeeping—and Sister Marie persists in writing in all these items, and following them with a prayer, especially when she is given sausages and wants bandages. Watch out for your petticoat.'

'Does she get them? Bandages, I mean?' Yvette was unsure whether he was joking or not.

Marc shrugged. 'The hospital's been operating for more than twenty years. It speaks well for trust in God.'

Madame Brun-Cartier chose that moment to wake fully. 'Trust in *le bon Dieu* is never misplaced. Young people nowadays don't understand that.'

Yvette didn't know how to reply to this but Marc was unruffled. 'Ah, Madame, how are you feeling now? You're looking much better than the last time I saw you.'

Madame Brun-Cartier smiled. 'Do you think so? They never tell me what's wrong with me—only that I'm worn out and must rest. That's all I do—rest. But they're very kind to me here. I shall remember them in my will.' She looked round as though to make sure no one was listening. 'I won't tell them, though. This way I'll keep them on their toes.'

Marc rose to his feet. 'I shall leave you two to discuss it. As for me, I have a bag of apples to give Sister Marie. *Adieu.*' His hand rested on Yvette's shoulder. 'I'll come by again. *Bonjour, Madame, Mademoiselle,*' he bowed to both and left.

Madame Brun-Cartier, now thoroughly awake, wanted to talk. 'Don't trust that young man,' she told Yvette. 'He's too smooth, too sure of himself. He thinks I'm an old fool and you're a young one. Well, are you?' her eyes were surprisingly shrewd. 'Going to hop into town, are you—at his bidding?'

'I can't,' mourned Yvette.

Madame Brun-Cartier gave a cackle of laughter.

'You don't believe me. You'll find out for yourself. Sister Marie sometimes goes to collect groceries in a little cart. If you're set on getting there, you could do worse than ask her.' She closed her eyes.

Yvette sat there thinking. If Sister Marie were going tomorrow and would take her, that would be fine, but just suppose she were going only a week next Thursday, that was too long to wait. She closed her own eyes and in the hot afternoon drifted into a fantasy of herself pushed in a wheel-barrow over uneven ground by Captain Renaud. He was going faster and faster and jostling her about—and it was a different nun shaking her and saying, 'I've brought you a drink of milk and some bread and jam, and when you're finished we'll get Madam Brun-Cartier back to bed and you can see the babies.'

When Yvette helped Sister Marie with the accounts that evening the young nun laughed and said they had received sausages, cabbages and tur-nips this week and even some apples, and some wild honey.

'We bake our own bread,' she told her, 'and Sister Anne in the kitchen does wonders. We have two cows and some chickens and a small vegetable garden, and the maple trees we tap for syrup.'

When asked if she ever bought in the town, Sister Marie sighed, 'Not very often, I'm afraid. I went last week for the cabbages—ours aren't ready yet. Someone lent me a horse and a cart and we col-lected some beds too. Never mind, we manage somehow. I expect you'd like to see the shops. Perhaps one of your friends from the ship will call and take you out.'

'Perhaps,' Yvette agreed not too confidently, 'but they all have new husbands.'

Sister Marie seemed to find that amusing, which surprised Yvette in a nun.

It was clear to the girl that she was going to have to solve the problem of seeing the materials for herself. An idea began to form in her mind. She borrowed pen and paper from Sister Marie. A girl who could write could make things happen.

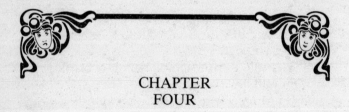

CHAPTER
FOUR

YVETTE was sure Pierre Michelin would come to the hospital with materials to show Madam Brun-Cartier, for her note to him had used that lady's name, but she had no idea when he would turn up. She waited impatiently all morning, undecided whether to take Madame into her confidence or not but Madame was in such a mood that she couldn't bring herself to do so.

A lunch of home-made sausage and vegetables with an onion gravy reinforced her natural optimism and after it she settled on the veranda with the old woman.

She had hardly begun to win a smile from that frosty character before Captain Renaud joined them there. Drat the man. Yesterday she would have been pleased to have seen him. But he had kept his promise. In spite of her misgivings she found satisfaction in that.

He was cheerful and confident. He put his hand on Yvette's shoulder and let it rest there, and that warmth that he alone seemed to arouse in her was there again. She wanted to put her hand on his and keep it there. She couldn't explain that to herself.

'Do you like chocolates?' he asked.

When they both replied that they did, he drew a little bag out of his pocket and handed it to Yvette. 'Share these out, then.'

'How kind of you,' she exclaimed. 'I don't know how long it's been since I had a chocolate.' She offered one to Madame, who took two, but Alain refused. The girl popped one in her mouth and ate it slowly, savouring it. Would he have brought one of his men chocolates?

Alain pulled a chair along and joined them.

Yvette was very conscious of his presence there as she introduced him to Madame.

'It's strange,' the old lady observed, starting on her third sweet, 'how young men appear from nowhere with gifts. Yesterday it was apples for the hospital, sweets for us today. I know they don't come to see me. Yvette is the only marriageable single girl in all Ville-Marie de Montréal. I think I may look forward to a swarm of lovelorn males with pleading eyes and charming gifts.'

'I am pleased you are here, Madame,' he told her. 'You will be able to direct Mademoiselle Deslauriers' attention to the right type of man, for, you understand, I wish to see her suitably settled before long.'

Yvette was incensed. Who was this Captain that he felt he must organise her life and even talk to Madame Brun-Cartier as though she were not there and not capable of sensible decision for herself.

Seething, she heard him ask who had come yesterday.

'Marc Barbier,' she replied. 'Wasn't that friendly of him to come so soon to see how I fared and to bring me news of the other girls?'

'Yes,' he agreed, but he frowned.

'That doesn't please you,' Madame Brun-Cartier cackled. 'Monsieur Barbier is a well-set-up young man and is of a good family and Yvette knew him in France, I believe. He might well take a wife. Are you married, Captain Renaud?'

Alain shook his head, but Madame went on. 'Yvette would do very well for you,' she told him, 'young, pretty, and willing.'

Yvette's cheeks were fiery red but she did not protest. She felt she should. She wouldn't even consider him as a husband. But she waited for his answer, carefully avoiding his eyes.

'Mademoiselle is meant for a settler's wife,' his voice was cold.

'Ma foi,' the old woman rocked in her chair, 'you sound very cool—and yet you brought her chocolates. Never thought of becoming a settler? The King gives good grants for army officers to remain here. 'There's some girl back in France,' she prodded.

'No.' Alain shook his head.

'The girl's in Québec,' Yvette thought to herself. Hadn't Marc said something about a girl called Hélène? Alain made no mention of her. 'The army's been my career,' he went on.

'And where will that lead?' the old woman was scornful. 'Death or wounds on a muddy field somewhere, and all the excitement over.'

'Come, Madame,' Alain began, but he never finished because footsteps approached along the veranda and a deep male voice called out, 'Madame Brun-Cartier?'

'Good God, another one,' whispered Madame, her gaze on Alain. 'This one asks for me.' She bestowed a smile on the newcomer. 'Monsieur Michelin, how kind of you to call on me.'

Monsieur Michelin had samples of materials over his arm. Though the day was nearly as warm as yesterday, he wore a jacket and a hat. He took off the hat and laid it on the veranda rail and revealed wavy brown hair worn in a braid. The hat was a tapabord with turned-up brim and silk lining. He wore knee-length capots of a fine grey wool.

'I was pleased to hear from you, Madame,' he bowed.

'Hear from me?' Madame raised her voice. 'I didn't send for you.'

Alain was looking at Yvette. He signalled to her to leave the two of them together, but Yvette had eyes only for the material.

'Monsieur Michelin,' she smiled at him, 'you have brought lovely materials. May I look?'

Madame Brun-Cartier shot her a shrewd look. 'Ah-ha, I understand, Monsieur Michelin has come to see me with his latest samples. If you are quiet, child, there's no reason why you can't stay and look—but there's no reason to detain the good Captain any longer.'

Alain was dismissed but he refused to recognise his dismissal. 'I shall be quiet too,' he promised. 'Proceed, Monsieur.'

So the materials were passed to Madame first, then to Yvette and last to Alain, and were examined carefully by all.

Monsieur Michelin was not put out. A pleasant young man, he was about the same age as Alain, but shorter and not so broad in the shoulders. His dark coat was of good quality material and fitted him a little snugly. 'So this is Pauline's husband,' Yvette reflected as she examined a green satin swathe. 'I like him'. She gave him a pleasant smile.

'I have cheaper materials too,' he assured Yvette as Madame fingered a heavy velvet. 'When Mademoiselle's leg is better perhaps she would care to visit the shop.'

'Visit the shop?' Madame Brun-Cartier found that inordinately funny. 'Mademoiselle doesn't need to visit the shop if you come to her.'

Monsieur Michelin was a little nonplussed by that but, a true salesman, he commented only on the piece of lace he held, pointing out how fine it was.

'Don't you have any lighter colours?' asked Madame.

'Yes, there are some lovely pinks and blues in the satin and a gold silk.' Monsieur Michelin was only a little daunted. 'I couldn't bring everything.'

'Hmph,' Madame muttered. She looked at Yvette. 'Satisfied, then?'

Yvette kept her expression bland, 'Perfectly, Madame, it was kind of you to let me look as well.'

Alain looked from one to the other. 'What are you two up to?' he asked.

Yvette looked away from him and she coloured.

'Questions, questions,' grumbled Madame. 'Can't an old woman think about a new dress without being taken to task?' She turned to Monsieur Michelin. 'Is that new wife of yours bred to the needle?'

'Bred to the needle?' echoed Monsieur Michelin, puzzled.

'Does she sew, man?'

'Unfortunately not well enough for your purpose, Madame,' he told her, 'but Madame Poitier is usually willing to oblige you ladies.'

'I know all about her,' was the grumpy reply. 'Well, I'll let you know. I like the look of the blue velvet but I am an old woman and Madame Poitier has raised her price to two crowns.' She closed her eyes.

Monsieur Michelin shrugged and gathered his samples together. If he was angry at this kind of treatment he didn't allow it to show. He glanced at Yvette. 'I believe you came over on the same ship as my wife. How is your leg?' His eyes were bright and assessing.

Yvette knew that Pauline had mentioned her to

him, but what had she said? Would she have retailed her mother's story?

As Monsieur Michelin was taking his leave there were more footsteps. This time it was Liliane, accompanied by a man. She nodded to Alain and Monsieur Michelin and embraced Yvette.

'I've brought my husband to meet the girl who saved my life,' she announced dramatically.

Yvette drew back a little, feeling all eyes upon her.

'Here he is,' Liliane went on, 'Paul Moreau.'

Paul kissed Yvette on both cheeks and exclaimed, 'I have you to thank for a brave deed.' He tenderly assisted her back into her chair, for she had risen to greet Liliane. Then he drew up a chair for his wife.

'Isn't he gorgeous?' whispered Liliane. 'And so kind to me.'

Yvette had to admit Paul was probably the handsomest man she had ever seen. Dark-haired with grey eyes and very even classical features, he was tall and perfectly proportioned. His teeth were white and regular, his expression pleasant. He was very impressive. His manners too were polished and easy. He bowed to Madame Brun-Cartier when Yvette introduced her and enquired after her health and managed to appear interested when she listed her symptoms.

'Paul has been hunting,' Liliane informed them, 'and has brought a turkey for Sister Jeanne and the patients.' She sank back in her chair. 'You must come and see the house. We're very comfortable.'

She prattled on telling Yvette about the good fireplace and the kitchen Paul had provided for her. Remembering Marc's comments, Yvette replied she'd love to come.

'The only problem is getting you there. The horse has cast a shoe,' Liliane frowned, 'and the cart has lost a wheel.' She appealed to Alain, 'Isn't it unfortunate?'

'Never mind,' he soothed, 'you'll soon have that put right.' There was no trace of a smile on his face but his eyes danced as they met Yvette's.

Madame Brun-Cartier murmured, 'Bridegrooms don't usually want company.'

Paul gave her a glance that was completely guileless, 'Oh Madame, how unkind you are.'

Liliane was full of news about the town and the other girls and told Yvette Paul had friends among whom she was sure to find a husband. The pair of them stayed twenty minutes, chatting all the time, and left shortly before Sister Marie brought a plate of bread and butter and the hot syrup drink of her own invention.

'Is it true you saved her life?' asked Alain, putting jam on bread.

'Yes, I suppose it is,' Yvette admitted. 'She was standing at the rail when the cargo ran loose and the rail was broken by its weight. But anyone would have done it—I just happened to be there.'

'Not anyone,' he corrected her. 'Only a brave girl with the wit to move quickly. You risked a good deal. A modest heroine as well,' he added.

'Now she has a husband—and you do not,' Madame pointed out. 'Life is unfair.'

But Yvette with the Captain's praise ringing in her ears and his approving eyes upon her was not so sure of life's unfairness. He had seemed much more likeable today.

When Alain had left after kissing her hand and holding it for a brief heady moment, Madame had more to say.

'*Tiens, ma jeune,* you've saved yourself a trip to the shop and seen your friend's husband. You might have told me what you were planning.'

'I'm sorry, Madame,' Yvette apologised. 'I wasn't sure how you'd take it.'

There was a silence. 'How did I take it?'

'Very well, Madame, you were quick to know what had happened and were kind to me. Would you like another chocolate?' She held out the bag.

Madame Brun-Cartier began to laugh. 'Yes, I would.' She pocketed the remaining sweets. 'They're my favourites.'

Yvette's mouth opened in protest, then closed again. They were her chocolates—or had been. She smiled ruefully as Madame pointed out that she had had what she wanted and closed her eyes. Perhaps Captain Renaud would bring some more or there would be others who would come to visit bearing gifts. Madame had said she was the only marriage-able single girl in Montréal. She had only to wait and the men would come to her. She began to feel a sense of power and of well-being. Today had been quite pleasant except for Captain Renaud and his air of owning her. She quite forgot she had valued his approval.

The following morning Sister Jeanne called Yvette into her office. 'I'm glad you've settled down so happily with us and that your leg is progressing well. Madame Brun-Cartier assures me you're a sensible girl.'

Yvette murmured that that was very kind of her, and wondered what was coming.

Sister Jeanne picked up a letter from her desk. 'I've had a note from Madame Archambault.' She paused.

Yvette looked at her blankly.

'Madame Archambault is lady-in-waiting and companion to the governor's wife. Her husband is aide-de-camp to the governor.'

Yvette nodded, since nothing else seemed to be expected of her.

'She has written to me,' the nun continued, 'requesting my permission for you to visit her this afternoon.' Sister Jeanne sat back and looked at the girl. 'I can see no objection to that. She promises to send a carriage for you and to return you the same way. It's very kind of her. She tells me your mother was a distant relative.'

This was news to Yvette. It must be Marc's doing. She tried to look like a girl who had relatives everywhere. 'Archambault?' she frowned. 'What was her maiden name?'

Sister Jeanne shrugged. 'You can explore the relationship this afternoon. The carriage will come after lunch, so be ready.'

Yvette took her leave of Sister Jeanne and went to offer her services to Sister Marie. She was very excited at the prospect of an outing and the young nun shared her pleasure.

'If she offers you any help for the hospital,' she suggested, 'our sheets are very thin—and very scarce.'

By two o'clock, Yvette was on the veranda, waiting. Madame Brun-Cartier came out to take up her position before the carriage arrived. Yvette had secretly been expecting something grand but it was a small, old, open carriage that came. Still the groom bowed to her and assisted her to seat herself. It was a decided improvement on the vehicle she had arrived in a few days ago.

'*Tiens*,' exclaimed Madame Brun-Cartier, waving her goodbye, 'you've gone up in the world.'

Considering the state of the carriage, Yvette wasn't quite sure how she meant this. Still she thoroughly enjoyed her drive through Ville-Marie. This time she could see everything, not like the first time when she had been in that terrible farm-cart.

As she passed the shops, she signalled to the groom to go more slowly so that she could see them. Actually there wasn't a great deal to see since only a few showed their wares outside and the doors and windows that fronted on the street were small anyway. In Michelin's there was material on display in the window and at the bakery there were loaves of crusty bread and cakes. There was a furniture shop and a chandler's and some which bore only the name of the proprietor. Yvette longed to explore them all but she had to content herself with the thought that an interesting afternoon lay before her.

The carriage wound its way down a hill and the river and the harbour could be clearly seen from here. *Le Poisson Bleu* was no longer there, but there were a few small boats—fishermen's, perhaps—and some canoes.

They stopped before a large stone house and Yvette was assisted down and to the front door. She raised the great knocker in the shape of a lion's head and was glad to pass from the glare of the sun into a cool entrance hall.

Marc was waiting there and he kissed her on the cheek.

'Was it you who sent for me?' she asked.

'In a way,' he smiled at her and put his arm around her waist. 'Are you pleased?'

'Pleased to be out of hospital,' Yvette balanced on her crutches, drawing away from him. 'What do you want?'

He laughed and led her down the hall into a sitting-room. 'Direct, aren't you? Have a comfortable chair,' he indicated a red plush armchair with a footstool. 'What should I want, except to see you?'

Yvette didn't like the way the conversation was

going. 'Where is Madame Archambault, or is there such a person?'

Marc stood looking down at her. 'Of course there is. She wrote the note . . . at my dictation.'

'Am I not to see her?' Yvette was impatient.

'Where's the hurry?' asked Marc. 'I thought you'd be glad of my company. After all, it was I who suggested you to her.'

'You still haven't told me what it's all about.' Yvette sat forward accusingly.

'Can't you guess?' Marc perched on the arm of her chair. 'You managed to get Monsieur Michelin and his samples to the hospital.'

Yvette was astonished.

He smiled at her. 'You wonder how I know. What did you think of his materials?'

'Very nice quality,' Yvette responded.

'I'm glad you agree.' Marc's eyes were dancing. 'Madame Archambault wanted to be sure.'

'She wants me to sew for her,' said Yvette. 'That's it, isn't it?'

Marc wouldn't give her an answer. He rose and went to the door. 'I'll tell her you're here.'

When Madame Archambault came into the room, Yvette started to rise but was motioned to stay where she was.

Madame was a beautiful woman, blonde with a fresh pink and white complexion. She was dressed in grey half mourning, which did not suit her. Her dress clung to her small waist and shapely figure. Yvette was sure she wore whalebone stays to give her that slim look. Madame's skirt was full from the hips and fell in flounces to the ankle. Her hair was arranged in a curly bang at the front and ringlets at the back. A woman of considerable style, she couldn't have been more than ten years older than Yvette, but she displayed such poise and sophistication that they might have been from a different world. She said she was in mourning for her father-in-law.

'Marc tells me you're a dressmaker,' she began as she arranged herself on a straight-back gold settee. 'Are you an experienced dressmaker?' She inspected Yvette closely. 'Your clothes fit well, your appearance is smart, but I'm looking for someone with that indefinable something—call it style or flair—do you have it?'

Yvette looked at Madame Archambault. Strangely, she didn't feel nervous, only excited. Here was opportunity indeed. 'You must judge for yourself,' she declared, 'but I know you would be interesting to dress. You have a good figure and you hold yourself like a queen.'

For the first time, Madame smiled. 'If your needle is as good as your tongue we'll be well suited. I shall tell you what I want. The governor is to hold a ball in three weeks' time and I shall be out of mourning by then. It's not the sort of occasion I should bother much with in France—after all, what real society is there here? But none the less I wish to look my best. I thought of silk or satin, something pretty to suit me. I understand Monsieur Michelin has new stock in. I fancy we might go and look at it. We can better agree a price for your work then.'

This was even better than Yvette had expected. Madame Archambault summoned the carriage again and Marc accompanied them.

Yvette thoroughly enjoyed the stir they created in the shop. Monsieur Michelin himself came forward to serve them and Pauline was summoned from the back to bring chairs and clear a space on the counter so that the material could be properly seen.

Yvette smiled at her graciously and got a frosty nod of the head in return.

Madame Archambault couldn't decide between pale pink silk and an ice-blue satin and asked Yvette and Marc for an opinion.

Monsieur Michelin tactfully withdrew a little while they discussed it.

'Neither, Madame,' said Marc. 'I would have neither of those.'

'Neither?' Madame was astonished and then amused. 'What would you choose?'

'That deeper pink silk over there,' he pointed to it. 'With your colouring, that will take all eyes, and the rosy pink will enhance that look of softness and elegance that is yours.'

Yvette nodded her head. Marc was absolutely right. She could begin to see the kind of dress that could be created from this.

Monsieur Michelin brought the rose pink nearer and the girl fingered it.

Without any more ado Madame agreed and it was left to Yvette to decide on the proper quantity to buy and the matching silk to sew with and ribbons. Monsieur Michelin was sheer pleasure to deal with for he knew exactly what she wanted before she even mentioned it.

Then he asked Pauline to prepare tea and serve them with little cakes as well. To be treated to tea, that expensive beverage, was a treat indeed. He promised to deliver the material to Yvette the following day.

Madame Archambault told Yvette she would send the carriage for her the following afternoon when she could expect to take measurements and show her the preliminary sketch of the new dress. Yvette was dropped at the hospital and Marc and Madame drove off together.

Yvette expected Madame Brun-Cartier to be waiting for her on the veranda eager to hear all about her expedition, but it was Captain Renaud who sat there.

He rose to his feet and motioned her to a chair and then sat opposite her. 'Did you enjoy your afternoon?'

'Oh yes,' Yvette was still bubbling over, 'Madame Archambault wants me to make a ball gown for her. We went to Monsieur Michelin's and picked the material. Marc said she should have rose silk. It will be beautiful.' Her voice became a little uncertain as she saw the Captain was frowning at her.

'Marc?' he queried. 'What does Marc have to do with this?'

She told herself it was none of his concern if Madame Archambault took Marc shopping with her, but how was she to make this army officer aware of that?

'It was Monsieur Barbier who suggested that I could make the dress and Madame Archambault wrote to Sister Jeanne about me going there. She said it would be all right,' she began reasonably.

'Ah yes,' agreed Alain. 'Madame claimed you as a distant relative; very distant, I should imagine.'

Yvette's eyes dropped before his. Since Madame Archambault had not discussed that relationship she hesitated to invent the connection, as she might mistake it. 'Quite distant,' she faltered.

The Captain might have pursued that but he chose another topic. 'Did you like Madame Archambault?' he asked.

'She was very pleasant with me.' Yvette was glad to be on safer ground and there was a good deal of enthusiasm in her voice. 'What a beautiful woman she is and so chic. When we went in the carriage she wore gloves to match her dress—gloves with drawstrings of silk. How agreeable it would be to have a life such as hers, to be able to call for a carriage, order a new dress, be waited upon.'

'You fancy that sort of life?' The Captain's voice was cold. 'Don't allow your mind to be filled with such ideas. It will not happen for you.'

'But there are rich people here,' Yvette protested. 'If I find a rich husband I might have a velvet cap such as Madame wore today, or even dresses of silk—silk such as I saw in Michelin's, or a house with crystal chandeliers. There were chandeliers in Madame's house and there was a serpentine table there and an armoire of sassafras wood.'

'The governor's house,' Alain pointed out. 'How do you come to know about such fine things?'

'My mother used to take me shopping with her,' Yvette softened, remembering those days. 'She loved good furniture and splendid carving and exquisite materials. She taught me about them.'

The Captain moved nearer. 'Well, well, you continue to surprise me. And that is what you want, a rich husband?'

With his hand on hers, sending quivers of pleasure up her arm, Yvette was not sure what she wanted. She looked into his eyes and found herself lost in them, so dark, so limpid, so fixed on her and yet she could not tell what he was thinking. She said nothing.

He asked again, 'Is it a rich husband you want?'

Yvette realised he still held her hand and she withdrew it. 'Why not?' she asked. 'I have come to do the best I can for myself.'

The Captain smiled, a grimace of the lips that did not reach his eyes. 'Don't take Madame for your model. I don't suppose she has a single idea in her head that isn't connected with preserving her beauty and conquering men.'

'If it weren't for women like that, dressmakers

would never make a living,' Yvette offered equably, wondering if Madame Archambault had tried to conquer the Captain.

'And that's another thing,' Alain continued. 'Are you talented enough, experienced enough, to make a ball gown for a society woman?'

Yvette felt as though he had thrown cold water over her. 'I don't know,' she admitted, 'but I'm going to try.'

'If you fail,' the Captain queried, 'what then?'

'I won't fail,' Yvette was suddenly confident. Why was this odious man trying to destroy her confidence? She struck back at him. 'When your superiors send you out against the Indians, do they ask you if you're going to win? And how you'll feel if you don't?'

Alain began to laugh. 'I'd sooner go out against the Indians than argue with you. So long as you're confident about it I see no reason why you shouldn't make the dress. Have you agreed about a price for your work?'

'Not yet,' Yvette bit her lip. 'I shall do a sketch tonight and then tomorrow I'll show it to Madame Archambault. If she likes it, I shall know how much work is involved.'

'That's sensible,' he applauded, 'but mind she does not try to cheat you. Ask Madame Brun-Cartier what is reasonable to charge.' He rose to his feet. 'I wish you well.'

Yvette was surprised by that. She didn't quite understand why he was now so helpful.

Alain bowed over her hand and bent to kiss it. She was almost sure he had meant to kiss it and already felt that anticipatory thrill that his touch invariably aroused in her when he frowned and dropped it so that it fell back into her lap.

His nose wrinkled in what Yvette decided was distaste. 'I needn't ask if you're still using the bear grease. I can smell for myself that you are.' His hand brushed her shoulder as he passed her chair. '*Au revoir, Mademoiselle.*'

'*Bonjour*, Captain Renaud,' she called after him icily. 'I cannot help the smell.' She wondered why she allowed him to make her so angry.

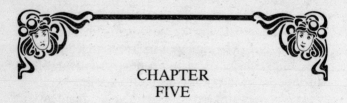

CHAPTER
FIVE

By morning Yvette had completed her sketch, shown it to Sister Marie and was helping her to bath the babies. This could be managed as a sitting-down job and both Yvette and Sister Marie enjoyed it. They had nearly finished when Yvette was summoned to the door.

Monsieur Michelin himself had brought the material and he wanted to deliver it to her personally. She stood in the hallway talking to him and was astonished when he dived into his pocket and begged her to accept a small gift.

Yvette opened the little package he gave her and exclaimed in pleasure at the two little combs inside. The hilts were fat little cherubs delicately carved in light wood and the combs were designed to fit snugly into the hair. They just asked to be placed there and the girl pushed one into the loose curls above her right ear and admired the effect seen in her reflection in the window.

'But why?' she asked, still fingering its mate. 'I have done nothing to earn it.'

Monsieur Michelin smiled, 'You are a new customer. I look forward to a happy business partnership. It has long been my desire to expand my fine fabrics section. I see a great market there as the town develops. Why should we be tied here to Paris styles and dresses made there?'

'It's very kind of you, Monsieur,' murmured Yvette, excited at the thought of establishing a dressmaking business.

'My wife and I shall always be pleased to do whatever we can for you,' Monsieur Michelin told her.

Yvette concealed a smile and wondered what he had promised Pauline for such an undertaking.

'Come in and see us again,' he urged. He left on that note.

Madame Brun-Cartier then signalled to Yvette and she was shown the combs.

'Hmph,' was her comment, 'I hope his wife knows what he's up to.' She brushed the subject aside. 'I'll give you some money and when you're out this afternoon get the carriage to stop at Leger's and buy me some coconut sweets and some chocolates. The driver won't mind waiting if you ask him nicely.'

Yvette readily agreed to this, though it was couched as a command rather than a request. Sister Marie too wanted something from the shops and Yvette was glad to have a reason to go into them and some money to spend.

After lunch, she was pleased to see the carriage waiting for her. This time, it was a closed carriage with a small crest on the door. It was black and newer-looking than the first one had been.

The same groom, a pleasant youngish man, helped her in and shut the door and she found herself seated comfortably on dark wine plush. She felt considerably more important in this vehicle.

The fitting with Madame Archambault went well and she declared herself well satisfied with the rough sketch Yvette had made. With some trepidation the girl introduced the subject of payment and there followed a brisk discussion.

Yvette, primed by Madame Brun-Cartier, wanted two crowns. Madame Archambault offered one crown, fifty livres, exclaiming, 'You are only new here. I am giving you a start so the price should be low.'

Considering that for a moment and wondering how much she would be charged for making up her fur jacket, Yvette compromised, and they agreed on one crown seventy-five.

Elated that she would be able to tell Captain Renaud about this bargaining and feeling she had handled it quite well, Yvette was soon back in the carriage and on her way to the shops.

Leger's proved to be a delightful little sweet-shop and while she was there, Liliane came in to buy some chocolates. As Yvette was being served Liliane pinched a sweet from the counter and put a finger to her lips enjoining secrecy.

Yvette smiled and said nothing.

When they were outside the shop she didn't mention it, for Liliane took hold of her arm and exclaimed, 'It is nice to have someone to shop with.

Let's go to Michelin's and look at everything. Lucky Pauline, there's nothing I'd like better than to have a shop.'

Yvette handled her crutches neatly and the two of them entered Michelin's, which was only a few doors away. Pauline was serving a customer and another was waiting so they had a browse round, admiring the stockings, the ribbons, the skirt stiffeners called *criades*, some new cotton ginghams. Yvette held up a *considération*, a pannier to be worn over a skirt, and wished she had some money to spend.

'You should see the wine shop,' said Liliane. 'Paul bought a bottle of red wine there the day we married and we drank it that first evening. It was good. We were both a little tipsy.'

'Lucky you,' sighed Yvette. 'You have a husband to buy you things.'

'Yes, I have a husband,' agreed Liliane, 'but where did you get those darling little combs you're wearing in your hair?'

'They were a present,' answered Yvette.

'A present? Who from?' Liliane was clearly impressed. 'Look,' she whispered, 'aren't there some like them over there?' She began to examine a selection of combs and slipped one just like Yvette's into her hair. So swift was her action and so unexpected by her that Yvette couldn't believe it for a moment, but a second comb went into the other side of Liliane's hair.

It was unfortunate that Pauline chose that moment to finish with the second customer and come towards them. 'Are you buying the combs?' she asked pleasantly.

Yvette shook her head but Liliane quickly removed the combs she had placed in her fair curls. 'Just trying them,' she murmured. 'Perhaps Paul will buy them for me.'

Pauline looked at Yvette, waiting.

'These are mine,' Yvette protested, feeling her glance.

'They were a present,' Liliane broke in.

'Oh yes?' Pauline's tone had an edge. 'A present from whom, Mademoiselle?'

It was on the tip of Yvette's tongue to reply, 'From your husband', but she hesitated, remembering Madame Brun-Cartier's words. She had no desire to make trouble between husband and wife. If she made Pauline look foolish it would only revive the animosity between them—and the old gossip about her mother. No, no, better to keep quiet about the giver.

'There were five pairs like this only this morning,' Pauline's voice was sharp. 'Let's count them, shall we?' She held up four sets of combs. 'You see there are only four now.'

Yvette wished the earth would open and swallow her but she would not even now give Pauline the satisfaction of returning the combs. They stood glaring at each other.

'Tell her I had them in my hair when I entered the shop.' Yvette turned to Liliane.

'It's true,' Liliane agreed. 'I noticed them and asked her about them. I don't know why she won't tell you who gave them to her.'

'Perhaps because she can't,' snapped Pauline.

'What do you mean by that?' asked Yvette, now so angry that she was determined to stand her ground.

'I think you know what I mean.' There were two spots of bright red colour in Pauline's cheeks. 'I suggest you can't tell who gave them to you because you took them.'

'Girls, girls,' Monsieur Michelin broke in, coming from the back of the shop, 'what's the fuss all about? I heard you as I came in. Whatever will Captain Renaud think of you?' He turned to the Captain, who had followed him in. 'We've just been discussing a system of alarms for Indian raids.'

If Monsieur Michelin had hoped to deflect Pauline by this he failed dismally, for she immediately brought up the subject of the combs. 'There were five pairs of these here this morning.' She waved the offending sets at her husband.

Yvette was watching his expression. Consternation and guilt were written there. Quite obviously, he hadn't told Pauline.

'Ah yes,' he exclaimed softly, 'but I sold a pair this morning—for a present, I believe.' He eyed the combs in Yvette's hair, 'And *très chic*, very becoming they are, Mademoiselle,' he bowed to her.

Pauline's mouth opened and closed again without a word.

'I would have told you if I'd thought it was

important.' Monsieur Michelin's voice implied he didn't have to explain his actions to her. 'Perhaps you should apologise about the misunderstanding.'

Pauline flushed and murmured, 'I'm sorry I was mistaken, Yvette,' in a stiff tone.

Yvette shrugged. 'I'm glad it's been explained.' She looked at Monsieur Michelin as she spoke. Both of them knew it hadn't been properly explained.

'But who bought them and gave them to Yvette?' asked Liliane plaintively.

No one answered that question though Yvette felt Captain Renaud's eyes on her as well as Pauline's.

'And why is it such a secret?' Liliane went on.

Yvette could have shaken her. Why couldn't she leave it alone?

Monsieur Michelin did his best to smooth it over. 'If Mademoiselle has a friend, an admirer even, there is no need to tell everyone, however curious we may all be.' He smiled charmingly. 'Was there some purchase you wished to make, Mademoiselle?'

'Yes,' Yvette was more than pleased to change the subject. 'Sister Marie wants some white net.'

Monsieur Michelin himself served her, watched by the others, so there was no chance for either of them to say anything.

Thankfully, Yvette limped out, bidding them all good day. She was surprised when Captain Renaud followed her out.

'I shall accompany Mademoiselle to the hospital,' he told the groom, and his statement was accepted without question.

Yvette suddenly wished desperately that the open coach had been sent for her today. This one was too enclosed, too warm. She hadn't noticed it before but now she found her cheeks were flushed, her dress sticking to her. Besides it was small, capable of seating only two on the single bench, and Alain took up a good deal of room.

Yvette pressed herself against the side but she was very conscious of his presence, of his arm touching hers and, even as the coach swayed, of his thigh pressing against hers. As they rounded a corner, she felt his knee against her own, strong and bony. He reached out lazily and pulled one of the combs from her hair.

'What are you doing?' gasped Yvette, her hand smoothing her curls.

'Just examining the cause of the trouble.' Alain turned the comb over and traced the fat cherub with his forefinger. 'Engaging little chap, isn't he?' he observed, smiling. 'And was the giver just as engaging?' He shot the question at her.

'Yes, no,' Yvette replied, and then realised what he meant. 'It wasn't anything like that,' she protested.

Alain's eyes were full of laughter and in the cramped space of the carriage very close to the girl's. 'Like what?' he drawled.

'Like you seem to think,' Yvette replied angrily.

Her hand reached out for the comb but though their fingers touched and a sharp tingle swept through her at that touch, Alain held the comb just out of her reach.

'May I have my comb back?' she asked coldly, marvelling at the evenness of her voice when the very presence of the Captain beside her was upsetting her and sending messages of alarm—and pleasure—from that fleeting contact of fingers.

'I think not,' he replied.

Yvette bit her lip. 'It's mine,' she protested, wanting to snatch it from him but well aware that his strength was superior to hers and that in any struggle he must be the victor. She wouldn't give him that satisfaction. She closed her lips firmly and retreated as far as possible into her corner. At least he didn't make any remarks about bear-grease scent. In fact he made no remarks at all.

Silence stretched between them. There was only the noise of the wheels on the cobbles and their own breathing.

Alain broke it. 'I'm waiting,' he told her. 'I want the whole story. Who gave you the combs?'

Yvette was stubbornly silent. Her eyes flashed at him. She knew it was foolish not to tell him. It was mostly the thought that he wouldn't believe her that held her back.

A look of anger flashed into Alain's eyes and her own dropped. He put his hand on her wrist and pulled her towards him. 'Your silence tells me a great deal,' he whispered against her hair, now disarranged by the absence of the comb and falling over her ear. 'It tells me you are hesitant to name him. What did you have to do to earn them?' His voice was caressing but his arm was now around her waist, holding her tight against him.

Yvette felt her heart racing and her breath caught in her throat at the lean hardness of his body. She strove to free herself but was held fast. 'Why do you always think the worst of me?' she demanded.

'I, think the worst of you?' his lips tickled her ear. 'I didn't for one moment believe you had stolen the combs,' he objected. 'A girl like you receives gifts. She has no need to help herself to pretty ornaments. Did you struggle when he held you?' The Captain's voice was icy with contempt and Yvette shivered as he pressed her closer still.

'There was no struggle.' Yvette was now so overpowered by the closeness of his body that she could scarcely think coherently. 'They were a gift. You have no right to question me like this. I am not one of your soldiers.'

The Captain began to laugh and she could feel the laughter rising in his chest and spreading to his mouth, but there was no laughter in her. He relaxed his hold. 'Do you think I am not well aware of that,' he asked softly, 'or must I show you? You need another lesson.'

'I don't know what you mean.' Yvette, remembering full well that first lesson, faltered and seized the opportunity offered by this softer mood to put her hand on his left one. Her fingers closed on her comb before they were firmly held by both of his. 'Oh no,' he exclaimed, 'I shall not give it up so easily. What you did for Marc you must do for me. It was Marc who gave them to you.'

'No, no,' Yvette denied it, but clearly he did not believe her.

Suddenly he released her and rose to pull the curtains over the windows of the carriage. She was astonished by this action.

Why was it taking so long today to get back to the hospital, Yvette asked herself in that moment as the vehicle seemed to crawl up a slight incline.

'Come, I claim a kiss,' the Captain drawled, his eyes dancing with mischief in the gloom of the carriage as he returned to his seat.

'You may claim it,' retorted Yvette, her anger thoroughly aroused by his behaviour. She had been right to tell him nothing. He believed what he chose to believe—well, let him. What did she care? 'I shall not kiss you,' she declared with some complacency.

The Captain's eyes turned steely. In one quick movement he lifted her from where she sat and she found herself on his lap, held powerless there.

Her eyes opened wide in fright. 'I'll scream,' she told him, struggling against his chest while to her dismay and shame every instinct in her yearned for his embrace. Ever since that first time he'd kissed her she had wanted him to do it again. What magic spell had he cast on her? She hated him.

His lips fastened on hers, effectively silencing the threatened scream locked in her throat. His mouth was hard and demanding, forcing her lips open to receive his kiss, and her traitor tongue slipped past his teeth and tasted the freshness of his mouth. Of their own accord her captive arms stole around his neck and the curtains at the windows swung free, dancing in time over the dirt road to the throbbing music loose in her veins.

The carriage came to a standstill and abruptly he released her, tumbling her back to her own section of the bench.

'Here, take your comb'—he thrust it into her hand—'and tidy your hair,' he instructed, rising to his feet and picking up her crutches as the groom alighted and his hand fumbled at the door.

Shaken to her very depths, Yvette's hands trembled on the comb, trying to place it into her hair again. Her breathing was uneven. Even her good leg was unwilling to support her when she tried to stand.

Alain had to help her to alight and he carried her down the step and on to the path. With one hand he propped her up, and with the other he adjusted her crutches as the carriage drove away.

'Shall I help you in?' he asked, totally at ease.

'No,' she replied directing a look of loathing at him. 'I can manage on my own.' How unfair it was that he appeared totally unmoved by that fierce kiss while her whole being quivered at the memory. What must he think of her that he could close the curtains of the carriage and kiss her as insolently as he would kiss any common woman? And she had kissed him back, welcoming him, wanting more. She had been shamed by him, she told herself, but a tiny honest voice within her echoed, 'not shamed by him, shamed by my own body, by my desire for him.' She stilled that voice and snapped at him, 'Good afternoon, Captain Renaud.'

He put his hand on her arm and prevented her moving. His eyes rested on her speculatively. 'You would have done better to confide in me,' he told her softly.

'Let me go,' she cried, trying to wrench herself away.

His other hand came out to balance her as her crutches slid on the earth of the path.

'Temper, temper,' he chided, 'but already there is more of the woman in your reaction to me.' He smiled at her suddenly, and kissed her hand. 'You are beginning to leave girlhood behind, perhaps too quickly. Good afternoon, Mademoiselle Deslauriers, I shall find out, you know, who this man is.'

Yvette stamped her foot. 'There is no man in the way you mean.' She turned from him as he released her and hobbled to the door.

She reached her room without meeting anyone—for which she was grateful. She was still seething with anger and with hurt. Who did this Captain Renaud think he was anyway? There was no reason to care what he thought about her. He was opinionated, fierce and he had kissed her thoroughly, demandingly and turned her into a weak, trembling creature wanting to be kissed again. Her face burned at the memory of that kiss. The tears came and she lay down on the bed and cried her heart out.

She wasn't sure why she cried. She wanted to tell someone about it. Perhaps if she could have talked it over with her mother . . . She cried harder at that. She was alone. There was no one to turn to. If she told the nuns, they would say it was her fault. If she told Marc, he would laugh and spread the story in the town. Eventually she dried her eyes and washed her face, determined to put the whole thing behind her, straight out of her mind, but that was easier said than done.

She got out her mother's scissors, and that comforted her a little as she spread the new material over the table. She would cut out Madame Archambault's dress before the light failed.

An hour's careful work and the task was accomplished. She had a meal of cold turkey and salad in the kitchen with the nuns and went to bed somewhat cheered. No one remarked on the tear-stains.

The following afternoon as Yvette was sitting on the veranda piecing the dress together, Marc arrived.

'What's this I hear about you having an unknown admirer who showers you with combs?' he asked as Madame Brun-Cartier's head nodded.

'Now where did you hear about that?' Yvette touched the combs still defiantly in her hair. She sighed in exasperation.

'Your friend Liliane was only too eager to tell me when I saw her yesterday evening. She seems to like the shops—but who can he possibly be—this admirer of yours?' Marc grinned at her.

'Can't we just drop the whole subject?' Yvette asked wearily.

Madame Brun-Cartier chose that moment to wake. 'I warned you he hadn't told his wife,' she said sharply.

'Hadn't told his wife?' Marc began to laugh. 'What married man are you involved with? Was it Monsieur Michelin? The old devil, why didn't you tell Pauline yourself?'

'I couldn't be so mean.' Yvette didn't want to talk about it, but the whole story came out piece by piece, even down to Captain Renaud's anger, but she did not mention his kiss.

'It won't do him any harm not to be in complete command of the situation.' Marc clearly thought the whole thing a joke. 'But the way Liliane is spreading the story, you're going to be known as the most exciting girl in Ville-Marie. Michelin won't dare tell his wife now. Are you sure he doesn't fancy you himself?'

'Of course not,' snapped Yvette. 'It was a friend-ly business gesture of good-will and he must be regretting it as much as I do.'

'I don't know,' Marc couldn't stop laughing.

'You're a very attractive girl even if you do have to hop around at the moment.'

It pleased Yvette to be considered attractive but she wanted to leave the subject of the combs. When she said so, Marc declared himself willing, and he added, 'I have another piece of gossip. Our Alain was buying a gift in the jeweller's this morning.'

'Why is that gossip?' asked Yvette. 'What kind of jewellery?'

'A silver bracelet,' Marc sat back in satisfaction. 'It can't be for himself, can it?'

'No, I suppose not,' Yvette admitted and she shrugged.

'Don't you wonder who the lady is?' Marc was watching her.

'Why should I care?' Yvette questioned in return.

Marc leaned back and looked at his hands. 'I just had this idea that you did, that you had a tender spot for the good Captain. Perhaps it's just as well if you don't. They do say the army are quick to make "arrangements".' He let the word hang in the air.

'Arrangements?' Yvette echoed. 'What sort of arrangements?'

'How old are you, Yvette? Seventeen? Eighteen? Old enough to know the ways of the world. "Arrangements" are usually made with married women. After all a soldier is a man, a real man, with a man's needs. How many available single girls are there in Ville-Marie, or in Québec for that matter? You know the answer to that—none—or they wouldn't bring in girls from France. Well then, an accommodating married woman is a friend indeed. The fair Hélène is married, but in Québec. Who can have caught his eye here?'

'You should have held your tongue,' Madame Brun-Cartier snapped. 'You've shocked her.'

And indeed, Yvette was shocked, not so much at the idea of the army making 'arrangements' as by the thought of Captain Renaud doing so. Hè had seemed to her a man of honour and integrity. She didn't want to believe it of him. And yet, it was a man of experience who had kissed her.

'I'll be bound soldiers aren't the only ones who make arrangements,' Madame Brun-Cartier observed tartly.

Marc shrugged. 'Men will be men—as you say, Madame.'

They looked at each other, but nothing further was said on that subject.

'I hear Alain is taking a patrol among the Algonquins.' Marc was determined to give the ladies all the news.

'To the Algonquins?' Madame was surprised. 'That sounds dangerous.'

'You forget the Algonquins are our allies,' Marc pointed out, 'and they've asked for the army to advise them on fortifying their villages.'

'Are they expecting trouble from the Iroquois, then?' Madame was deeply interested.

'There's always trouble from that quarter,' Marc said soberly, and Yvette looked up from her sew-

ing. 'They've been quiet for a while but the Algonquins are more likely to judge their mood than we
are. They're right in their path. Still, don't start
worrying too soon. It may well be just one tribe
making a show of strength to the other by saying,
"Look, I have powerful friends. They come to help
when I ask them." '

'I'm too old to worry about Indians,' Madame
Brun-Cartier declared stoutly.

'Captain Renaud brought soldiers from Québec
with him,' Marc pointed out, 'so Ville-Marie will
still be protected without him.'

'Good,' exclaimed Yvette, and she told herself
she hoped he would stay away a good long time.
She put her hands to her lips and felt again that
bruising kiss of yesterday, his hard possessive arms
about her, his body taut against hers. She didn't
want him to die—if only he would just not return
until her leg was out of splints and she had chosen
her husband. That would suit her very well.

Marc said his goodbyes and Madame Brun-
Cartier went back to her room, but the girl remained, her sewing in her lap, her thoughts on the
army officer. She certainly didn't expect to see him
again before he left, and without a shadow of a
doubt didn't want to.

Why then did her heart beat faster when she
heard the Captain's footstep on the veranda? Hur-
riedly she gathered her things together, noting only
that he wasn't in uniform. She had no intention of
staying there on her own with him.

She had begun to rise when he put his hand on her shoulder.

'No, don't go. I want to speak to you.' His words were quiet.

She looked up at him, conscious of the gentle tone, and staring in spite of herself at his clothes. He was wearing leather jerkin and breeches. In the soft brown of the deerskin, he was magnificent. His shoulders were broader, his waist and hips leaner than they appeared in his blue uniform. His fair hair was worn loose about his shoulders instead of in the thick braid at the back of his head. He seemed younger, different, more alive, in this outfit. She could picture him gliding through the forest on the track of some mighty buffalo or bear.

Yvette sat again, but on the edge of her chair, poised for flight.

'I want to tell you I was mistaken about who gave you the combs,' he told her. 'Monsieur Michelin has confessed; he didn't speak up yesterday because he hadn't told his wife then.'

Captain Renaud sat on the bench opposite her. 'I'm sorry,' he added.

In the face of such directness, the words of protest which had been hovering on Yvette's lips were silenced. She had been prepared to warn him that she would never allow herself to be alone with him again.

'That won't take back your kiss,' she murmured and felt the hot colour mount to her cheeks.

'Would you want me to take it back?' he enquired softly. 'I had the impression you enjoyed it as much as I did.'

Yvette shook her head, not quite willing to deny enjoyment or at any rate participation. 'It was a shabby way to treat me.'

'Yes,' he agreed, 'I've said I'm sorry. Let's forget it and start afresh.' He smiled at her.

Yvette's rancour began to slip away. She didn't agree, but she changed the subject. 'Why aren't you in uniform?'

'I've been hunting. We've brought back a fine big deer. There'll be venison steaks tomorrow or whenever Sister Anne sees fit.'

'I've never had venison.' Yvette was suddenly interested. 'We had turkey yesterday and I liked that—and fried eels the other day.'

'Yes,' Alain was matter of fact, 'the hunting is fine and the good nuns are receiving many gifts of food. That's because of you.'

'People are being very kind.' Yvette nodded, not wanting to discuss reasons.

'Men, you mean, are coming to visit you.' The Captain stretched his legs along the bench. 'I've walked miles today. *Diable,* but I'm tired. It's a good tiredness. Whenever one of my men is in hospital, I've always added to the nuns larder. It's another mouth for them to feed.'

Yvette wasn't sure she wanted to be regarded as one more mouth. 'I'm not one of your men,' she informed him crossly.

'All the more reason to do it for my hoppity woman,' she was told.

'The hoppity woman you were meant to load with gifts and return,' Yvette exclaimed with some bitterness.

'What's the matter with you today?' Alain asked. 'You have a sharp comment or answer for everything. Aren't you feeling well?'

'Well enough,' Yvette snapped. All very well for him to dismiss that kiss. She couldn't forget how it had made her feel and the tears she'd shed last night. She couldn't understand why she was acting so brusquely when the Captain was doing his best to be conciliatory. She didn't want to be friends with him—that must be it. Every time she began to feel she might like him, he upset her. Besides, there was Hélène in Québec and the silver bracelet. 'I don't like to be called your hoppity woman,' she told him with as much dignity as she could muster. 'I am not your woman.'

'My responsibility, then,' he conceded lazily, making her feel he was amused by her reaction. 'My one-legged virgin.'

'I'm not yours,' she stormed.

'Nor any man's yet,' he retorted. 'What will you do while I'm away? Miss me? Wonder how I'm doing?'

'I shan't miss you,' Yvette was positive of that. 'I'll have no one looking over my shoulder to see what I'm doing, no one judging me.'

'No one caring what you do, no one wanting to help you,' he suggested softly.

'Is that how you see yourself, caring, helping?' asked Yvette, astonished and angry both. 'I can tell you I don't see you that way.'

'Foolish little girl,' he chided, not moving from his languid pose. 'I've brought you some more bear grease. You must nearly have finished that first lot.'

Yvette grimaced at that. 'Thank you,' she murmured politely.

'You needn't make faces at me,' Alain sat up suddenly. 'Or talk to me with such a pretence of gratitude. I know perfectly well how you feel about that grease. Promise me you'll use it.' His eyes bored into hers.

'Very well,' she agreed reluctantly, wondering at his power over her. 'I'll use it.' She took the pot he gave her.

'And you'll behave yourself,' he added, his expression grim.

'I don't know what you mean by that,' she retorted, vibrating with anger.

He put his finger under her chin. 'No more kisses for combs.'

In spite of herself, Yvette responded to that touch and she felt a wave of colour spreading to her cheeks. 'I gave no kisses,' she cried, trying to escape his finger, 'except to you—and only because you forced me.'

A slow smile softened his mouth. 'Forced?' He shook his head. 'You gave them willingly enough.'

He put his hands on her arms and everything in her wanted those hands to stay there but she shook herself free and found him laughing at her.

'I won't tease you any more.' He sat back with arms folded and regarded her, a twinkle in his eye. 'Well, *ma petite*, it's time I left. We set off for the Indian village tonight. Won't you wish me well?'

'Do you need my good wishes?' she asked, ruffled by those steady dark eyes searching hers.

'No, I don't need them,' he withdrew a little, 'but it would be nice to have them.'

'There is no danger, is there?' Yvette answered her own question. 'No, for Marc says . . .' she began.

He interrupted her, 'Ah yes, Marc says—Are you one of those women who must quote the man she's fond of?' There was a trace of sadness on his face. 'Do you ever exclaim, "Captain Renaud says", or even "Alain says"—but no, I see you don't.' He laughed, a bitter sort of laugh. 'No, I can hear what you would say of me, "Captain Renaud says I must use the bear grease" '—he imitated her voice so well that she had to laugh.

She put her hand on his knee in the first spontaneous gesture of reaching out to him that she had ever made. 'You must have heard me say it. Never mind, I *do* hope you and your men will return in safety.'

'Me and my men,' he commented dryly. 'I was hoping for something more personal—but that will have to do.'

A dimple appeared in Yvette's cheek as she smiled. 'Soldiers protect us all. I had to include your men.'

He took his leave without another word and Yvette felt somehow that she had disappointed him. What had made her so perverse, so ungenerous, that she could not have wished him well warmly and naturally when that was so obviously what he had wanted? There had been something almost pleading about him and yet she had refused to admit it, or having guessed at it had refused to acknowledge that the Captain might be human enough to want her sympathy, her friendly farewell.

He might not come back, she reminded herself. Why had she not given him a kinder goodbye? She upbraided herself for her churlishness. True he had behaved badly towards her in the closed carriage— she felt again his warm, demanding, lips on hers, and that hot pulsing langour it had roused in her—it was the shame of knowing her response to him that made her resent him. That was no excuse for meanness on her part. And she had been mean to part so with him. She felt the weight of her guilt.

She sighed and wished she could have that hour over again. He would be gone tonight. She had thought she would be glad of that. Why was it that she wasn't? He had somehow turned things around so that she was in the wrong when he had been the one who had misjudged her. She must put him out of her mind.

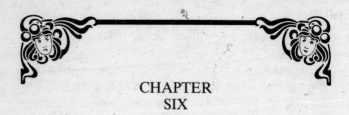

CHAPTER
SIX

FOR THE first few days Yvette relaxed completely.
It was wonderful, she told herself, to be rid of the
irksome attention of Captain Renaud. Of course
she wished him well in his mission to the Indians.
That went without saying. Everyone who lived in
Ville-Marie must do that and even offer a prayer to
the Virgin for the safe return of both him and his
men. There was no need to worry. Sister Marie had
said so.

It was good to be in the hospital—he had been
right about that—and to be meeting so many new
people. It seemed to the girl that this new life was
vastly different from what she had known in
France. With her mother in those good old days she
had had a place in the workroom and there had
been women coming for fittings passing on the
gossip of the town, and there had been neighbours,
of course. Here, she was a part of life itself. The
hospital was the centre.

The babies were born here, mostly to girls of
Yvette's own age—girls who had come to claim the
King's Dowry as she herself had. She could talk to
them and immediately had something in common

with them. She made friends with them, admired their babies, helped Sister Marie with the baby clinic which she held for all the little ones of Ville-Marie. She struggled over the accounts with her and provided in the mornings, at least, an extra pair of hands.

Yvette had developed a great facility with her crutches now that she no longer had to balance herself against the motion of sea and ship.

In the afternoons, she rested on the veranda, sewing and playing hostess with Madame Brun-Cartier to the callers who came.

It was very pleasant and satisfactory. True, when she looked at the silent green woods which lay behind the hospital and the blue sky above it and thought of the raw huddle that Ville-Marie de Montréal still was after twenty-four years and 800 inhabitants, a wave of longing sometimes swept over her for the solid towns of France, the farms and fields neat and well cared for, the softer bluer skies. But she would never see those scenes again, never rest her eyes on fields of hay or grain spread as far as the eye could see, and towns so large and bustling that the people couldn't be counted or known. Ville-Marie was carved out of the wilderness—raw, unfinished, only its main street cobbled, and still it looked as though if men laid down their forks and spades the forest would invade it and take it back, claiming what was its own.

She had little time to dwell on times past or future. For the most part, the present engulfed her.

Gradually, as the week wore on, she found she missed the Captain. She listened for his step on the veranda. Sometimes she thought she heard his voice, but it was only another strange man. For, as though realising the officer wasn't there, all sorts of men took the opportunity to visit the hospital. Some had cut fingers or blistered hands. Sister Marie laughed about these casual wounds and allowed Yvette to help in what she called her self-inflicted-accident hour.

It was always men who came and they all looked at Yvette with friendly eyes—some too friendly. She began to feel they came to assess her value, her bed-worthiness. Some of their glances stripped her bare.

'I've never seen so many ham-fisted men,' Sister Marie exclaimed one morning. 'We'll soon be out of bandages and tearing sheets again to make a new supply. Heaven knows we have few enough of those. I don't want to be uncharitable but really most of these men should have been able to doctor their own cuts and bruises.'

Being an unworldly person Sister Marie voiced no conclusions as to why they came, but Yvette was left in no doubt. When the good nun's back was turned even for a moment the girl was patted or pinched by the so-called sufferer. Even one with a scratch on his forehead moaned that he felt weak and put his arm around her shoulder to steady himself. His hand slid to her breast as he closed his eyes and held fast to her.

As Sister Marie had gone to fetch more wych-hazel Yvette tried to shake the man away, but one of her crutches slid to the floor and she nearly lost her balance. She found herself supported by the patient, a rough-looking big fellow with black hair and black nails.

He opened one eye at her. 'Broken leg or not,' he was breathing hoarsely, 'I'd be willing to take you on. What do you say? I have a farm and a house.' He had her firmly in his grasp now, his other hand pressing her buttocks.

A feeling of absolute revulsion swept over Yvette and the more she struggled the tighter he held her. It had not been like this when Captain Renaud had held her in the coach, she couldn't help thinking as she fought him. She was helpless and frightened, in a panic begging him to let go, when Sister Marie returned and picking up the crutch from the floor tapped the girl's attacker a sharp rap on the shoulder with it which made him let go.

Yvette sank on to a chair and tried to calm her trembling arms and legs.

'Are you all right?' asked Sister Marie. 'I blame myself for leaving you.' She spread wych-hazel so liberally on the man's cut that he squealed with its sharpness and then she rubbed his shoulder where the crutch had caught him with evil-smelling linament.

After that, Yvette was very quick to keep out of reach of any male patient. But she wasn't safe from their glances which alternately begged and ravished her.

Not even on the veranda, sewing, was she left in peace. Liliane and Paul brought two friends—the brothers Albert and Jean Pinault. Both were *coureurs de bois*, good-looking men in their mid-twenties dressed, as Alain had been when she last saw him, in deerskin tunics and trousers fringed at the hems.

They teased her and flattered her, told her they'd dreamed of such a girl as she was when they were deep in the woods tracking game.

'No,' said Albert who was the elder, 'not in the hunt, but at the campfire in my solitary blanket with the flames leaping red and gold over a smouldering log before I fell asleep with the dark trees as sentinel, then, *tiens*, I saw your face smiling softly and your arms reaching out to me. Ah, Yvette, even your name is beautiful—but not so beautiful as your eyes and your hair.' He didn't seem to mind in the slightest that the others were listening, but Yvette blushed and liked his flowery way of complimenting her. Ah, if only Alain could take a page from his book. She checked the thought.

When they had gone, Yvette asked Madame Brun-Cartier what a *coureur de bois* was.

'Liked that Albert, didn't you?' She looked at the girl shrewdly. 'But such a one as he is a hunter, a trader, an explorer, a man who lives in the woods—loves the woods better than any woman. Like all *coureurs de bois* he is a man who has escaped from the regulations and rules of society and civilisation.'

Yvette was disbelieving. 'Are there such men here? Aren't they all settlers?'

Madame Brun-Cartier shook her head. 'Settlers pay taxes and follow the rules. *Coureurs de bois* want more freedom and are quick to take it for themselves. The typical "wood runner" gives up the hard struggle of the settler to wrest a living from his farm. He wants a better life, more freedom, more money. I don't say it's like this with the brothers Pinault yet, for they are bachelors, but your ordinary *coureur de bois* kisses his wife good-bye one night and slips off in his canoe under the moon and the stars to trade for furs with the Indians. He tells his wife he is doing it for the money, but the lure of the forests and rivers traps him. A year later, perhaps two years, he paddles back one night—heaven help his wife if she's had no warning. Then he sells his furs without taxes and is away again. Probably he has an Indian wife by this time and he goes back to her or finds another in a different tribe.'

Yvette's expression was incredulous. 'Doesn't his wife mind?'

Madame shrugged. 'Perhaps, perhaps not. Would you, if you were Albert's wife? In any case, what can she do? As long as he leaves her enough money she may be pleased not to be troubled.' She paused and looked at Yvette. 'Child, child, life isn't all roses, you know.'

Yvette sighed and reluctantly concluded the brothers Pinault wouldn't do for her, but couldn't help regretting that, because there was a bold mischievous look about Albert that attracted her greatly, and a laughing independence that called out to her.

Marie-Rose and her new husband Jacques came one afternoon bringing with them his brother, Guillaume. He was a ginger-haired boy of nineteen or so. He brought four rabbits for the table and settled himself happily beside Yvette, ignoring Madam Brun-Cartier completely. He was a great talker, a compulsive chatterer and told Yvette about hunting and canoeing, and offered to take her paddling on the river when her leg was better. He was full of enthusiasm for the life of Ville-Marie and was quick to say that one day very soon he would have his own place and his own house.

'He's nice, isn't he?' whispered Marie-Rose as they all left. 'Nearly as nice as Jacques. I can see he likes you. He'll come again.'

Yvette knew her friend would be very pleased for her if she made a match with Guillaume—and Marie-Rose would be pleased too to have her husband to herself.

Yvette did like Guillaume. He was a thoroughly pleasing lad. Yes, that was it—he was a lad only. A picture of the Captain imposed itself unbidden on her mind. The Captain was a man. Guillaume was a boy.

Madame Brun-Cartier too had her candidate—or rather candidates—for Yvette's hand. A wealthy woman, she owned businesses. Daniel managed the saw-mill for her, Nicholas, the brewery. Each appeared on a different day.

The girl found Daniel the more impressive. He came with a load of small offcuts of wood.

'They'll do against the cruel winter cold,' he said as he piled them in the shed on the side of the building.

When he had finished he stayed to talk. He was a tall, burly man with a ruddy complexion and wavy brown hair. Very cheerful, he soon had even Madame Brun-Cartier chuckling with his stories of Indians and the way they lived. He had traded in furs and spent one winter with the Hurons. 'Very lazy,' he called them. 'The men only hunted and all the rest of the work fell to the women. The girls at thirteen and fourteen were pretty and winning but by twenty or twenty-five they were worn out and looked old and fat. But it was a treat to watch them working on furs. They softened them with their mouths and turned out first-class pelts. They did beautiful bead-work on leather moccasins and dresses, and beads were their money.'

Yvette was fascinated by his talk. She wanted to hear more, but Madame had only contempt for the Indians. 'Savages, heathens,' was her comment. 'No better than they should be.'

Daniel grinned at her in his easy fashion and wanted to know how the French were superior when it came to morals.

'Hmph,' was her retort to that.

'They have their own code,' Daniel insisted,

'their own ways; and there's a good deal more freedom among their young people than we have. I found much to admire—as well as some things to dislike.'

'You came back to your own kind,' Madame was quick to point out.

'It's more comfortable with your own people,' Daniel replied. 'Besides I speak the French language better than I ever spoke Indian.' He turned to Yvette. 'I fancy a French girl for a wife.'

'How is it you haven't found one at the Choosing?' she asked.

'That's no way to find a wife,' he insisted. 'A man needs to get to know a girl first and see if he can discover a friend in her.'

'Friendship in a woman,' observed Madame. 'You're a strange young man looking for that in a woman.'

'Perhaps,' he agreed, seeming not at all put out. 'But in the long winter evenings a good companion—someone to talk to—would be very pleasant. What do you think, Mademoiselle Yvette?'

'I think you're right.' Yvette's smile lit up her face. She couldn't help but warm to Daniel.

He left them then, but came back to see them.

Nicholas from the brewery arrived the following day. Small, dark-haired and rather swarthy, he brought a string of fish for the nuns. He appeared very shy but he managed to bow and introduce himself to Yvette and to kiss Madame Brun-Cartier's hand in a very polite way. He discussed the weather, which was fine, he prophesied it would remain so. He told them very little about himself save that he came from the south of France and loved to fish. He assured Yvette he would be a rich man some day for he intended to buy Madame out—and his ale was very popular.

The conversation was largely left to the girl and the old woman, for Nicholas either felt small-talk was beneath him or he had none at his command.

When he had gone, Yvette laughed and said, 'What would one do with such a silent man?'

'A clever woman might do as she pleased,' Madame retorted. 'He only wants encouraging, bringing out of himself. He's quite right when he says he will be wealthy. He's ambitious and shrewd. He just hasn't learned to make the best of himself.'

'He's hard work,' Yvette declared.

'Any man is hard work if a woman doesn't care about him,' Madame pointed out. 'You're becoming choosy because there are so many men coming. Watch out you don't become unkind—things can change, you know.'

'Change how?' Yvette was stung by Madame's words.

'Just suppose another bride ship arrived—your followers might melt away,' Madame's voice was sharp. 'Never count on things or people remaining the same. They don't.'

Yvette bit her tongue and remained silent. Madame's words had gone home. Situations didn't remain the same. She knew that. Suddenly she wished Captain Renaud would return.

By the time she had Madame Archambault's dress ready for its second fitting there was still no news of him.

This time she took her sewing and her beaver skins, as Madame had asked to see them. The fitting went well. Madame Archambault declared herself very satisfied with the work so far completed and Yvette was pleased to accept the part payment Madame offered, and accepted her invitation to accompany her and Marc to the furrier's.

He was a small, wizened, man and he treated Madame very deferentially. When he had put the finishing touches to the hat she had ordered he was nearly as obsequious with Yvette. He complimented her on the quality of the skins and was quick to understand the style of jacket she wanted. He wouldn't hear of the lynx fur being used for trimming but insisted it must be saved for a hat, and he made her try on several in different furs and styles. Finally she was convinced, and then they began bargaining.

Marc and Madame Archambault joined in this, but the little furrier wouldn't give way to any appreciable extent.

Yvette knew it was going to cost too much and in desperation offered to sew the lining herself; so a price was agreed to the satisfaction of both parties.

Marc then insisted on treating the ladies to hot chocolate and they repaired to the back of the sweet-shop where there were several small tables and chairs for this very purpose.

It was cool here after the warmth of the sun and they were the only customers.

'Little cousin'—Madame Archambault had fallen into this habit of addressing Yvette. She said it now as the woman came with the steaming cups of chocolate. 'Little cousin, you will enjoy the cream in this.'

The woman who had brought the cups withdrew with a smile.

Yvette did enjoy her drink. It was light and frothy and delicious. She sipped it slowly and licked her lips.

'You're a hard bargainer,' observed Marc. 'I don't think I'd want to do business with you,' but he smiled as he said it.

'You'll have a beautiful jacket.' Madame Archambault was in an expansive mood. 'When you marry you'll have a little dowry of your own there. I hear you have several suitors now.'

'There are men who come to talk to Madame Brun-Cartier and me on the veranda of an afternoon,' Yvette admitted. 'I'm not sure that I'd call them suitors.'

Marc laughed at that. 'Though the old dragon is a widow, I think you can be sure those young men aren't courting her.'

'I don't know,' Yvette smiled. 'She especially liked the one who came with Liliane's husband—Albert was his name.'

The other two nearly choked on their drinks at that.

'What a sense of humour you have, cousin,' exclaimed Madame. 'I haven't laughed so much in ages. But be serious, isn't there one among them whom you favour? I hear Daniel, the saw-mill manager, is a fine strong man.'

'Yes,' Yvette agreed, loath to add anything to that. She didn't really want to discuss it.

But Madame was engrossed. She knew by name and by reputation all the men who had called on Yvette and was keen to list their good and bad points. The only one she didn't mention was Marc. She had a good deal to say about Captain Renaud.

'But he's in the army,' protested Yvette. 'He's not eligible.'

'Nonsense,' was the forthright reply to that. 'The Captain knows how to get round regulations.'

'The very man for you', Marc assured her with a wink, so she didn't know whether he meant it or not. 'He must be interested,' he went on, 'or you'd be married by now.'

'Captain Renaud would be a good catch,' Madame pointed out. 'A respectable family, though of course he's a younger son. He'll stay here after his tour of duty. The king gives land and money to any officer who does. Decide on him, little cousin, and your future will be rosy.'

To her consternation, Yvette felt herself blushing. 'He's away with the Indians.' She took

a drink of cocoa and ran her tongue round her
lips. 'I don't think I like him very much anyway.'

'Husbands don't have to be liked.' Marc grinned
at the girl and appealed to Madame. 'Do they,
Madame?'

Madame Archambault shook her head. 'They're
more to be endured.'

The look that flashed between Madame and
Marc made Yvette uncomfortable. She tried to
describe it to herself—understanding? sympathy?
No, it was more than that, but she couldn't quite
place it.

Madame went on to ask Marc what he thought
about the talk of the Indians attacking and Yvette
brought all her attention to that.

'I don't want to alarm you ladies,' he replied, 'but
I'm very much afraid they will attack.'

Madame put her hand to her mouth, and Yvette
experienced a chill of fear.

'There have been attacks before.' Madame was
pale.

'Are we really in danger?' asked Yvette. 'Right
here in the town?'

Marc nodded, 'Yes, all of us are. You probably
think of a band of Indians marching up on the town.
Am I right?' he asked.

Yvette's eyes were large and frightened. 'Yes,'
she breathed.

'It's not like that.' Marc shook his head. 'A single
Indian or maybe five or six braves decide on a raid

and they creep up on a single house and dispose of the occupants.'

'All of them?' Yvette didn't want to know, but she asked, 'All of them? Even the babies?'

'Sometimes they kill the babies, sometimes they take them back and bring them up as their own.' Marc spoke slowly.

Madame Archambault shuddered. 'I don't know which would be worse.'

'To be alive must be better than to be dead,' Marc shrugged. 'Besides, they love babies and are very good to them. A child who's adopted into the tribe can do very well.'

'I think it's horrible,' said Yvette.

'Let's not talk about it any more,' suggested Madame. 'We have brave soldiers to defend us.'

'All right.' Marc finished his chocolate. 'But keep alert and watchful—that's the best defence.'

They talked of other things, but Yvette determined to keep that advice in mind. She went back to the hospital in a serious mood and more worried about Captain Renaud than she had been before.

That evening she went early to bed, but during the night she became suddenly conscious of movement and activity in the hospital. Probably a mother-to-be arriving in a hurry, she told herself.

As she lay there listening it seemed to her to be more upsetting than that. There were people moving about and the sound of rapid talking and exclamations.

The hair on Yvette's scalp began to prickle. She

knew there was danger and disaster. She got out of bed and slipped her shawl over her nightdress.

Down the corridor she went. There was no one there. She crept to the little room where emergencies were brought and stood hesitating at the door.

The sound of moaning came to her and then a man's voice, broken, pausing. She could not distinguish what he was saying. She thought he was crying.

Yvette hovered at the door and found she was trembling with cold and fear. She couldn't go in. If Sister Jeanne were giving some sort of treatment she wouldn't be welcome.

Rooted to the spot, her feet refused to move. Propped up on her crutches she leaned against the wall, shivering.

Sister Marie opened the door and gasped in surprise. 'What are you doing here?'

'What's happened?' Yvette's voice was a croaking whisper.

'Indian attack,' Sister Marie hissed. 'Get some more bandages from Sister Jeanne's office. We're already low on sheets but we'll have to use them for bandages.' She thrust a key into the girl's hand and as Yvette swung herself along to the office Sister Marie followed her with a lighted candle.

'Is it bad?' asked Yvette as she unlocked the door with hands that shook.

'Very.' In the flickering flame of that small light, Sister Marie looked exhausted as she swept up sheets and net into her arms. 'And just a girl, your age or younger.'

Together they raced back. Sister Marie motioned Yvette to come in with her. 'Another pair of hands won't come amiss.'

Several candles were burning in that small emergency room and Sister Jeanne was standing, her hands red with blood, over a body on the table.

'It's no use,' she said, straightening up. 'There's nothing I can do. She's gone, poor little child.' She began to pray: 'Our Father who art in Heaven, hallowed be thy name, thy kingdom come, thy will be done . . .' Her voice trembled on the words and she moved away from the table.

Yvette had her first real glimpse of the body. In spite of the blood and the bandages she recognised the face.

'Marie-Rose,' she whispered, her voice a question, though she knew the answer. 'It's Marie-Rose—dead.' She could scarcely hear her own voice in that quiet room.

Someone came out of the shadows, Marie-Rose's brother-in-law, Guillaume. 'Butchered, you mean. Look at her,' he was shouting. 'I was fishing with Georges from next door—his wife's in here with a baby. Poor soul, but at least Georges died cleanly, not like this. I don't know why they didn't kill me too—just hit me and knocked me down. Why didn't we get back earlier? I might have saved her and my brother.'

'Or been killed with them.' Sister Marie tried to

put her hand on his arm, but he drew away. 'It was the soldiers coming who saved you.'

'Georges killed one of them before the other killed him. But she called to me. I heard her calling before I fell. When I came to, again Marie-Rose called and I could see she was still alive. I picked her up, just a little thing she was, and I carried her here thinking they'd save her somehow.' He stood there sobbing and Sister Marie went to him again. Sister Jeanne rose from her knees.

Yvette didn't wait to see what happened then. She couldn't stand any more. With a sob, she rushed out of the room to get away from that mangled horror that was Marie-Rose. Tears were streaming down her face. It was dark in the corridor but what did that matter? Her eyes were blinded anyway.

She cannoned straight into another body— a man's body, and his arms closed about her. Startled, shocked, thoroughly frightened, she struggled to free herself, her crutches falling to the floor with a crash. But still those arms held her.

'Yvette,' Alain Renaud's voice seemed to come from a great distance, 'you're safe with me.' She put her arms around his neck and lay against him so that he supported her whole weight.

It didn't surprise her in the slightest that he should be there when she most needed him. Cradled in his arms she was, as he had said, safe, and she sobbed her grief away.

Sister Jeanne came out into the corridor and

Yvette knew that Alain had explained that one of his men had been hurt and was waiting outside. She saw the nun lead him in, but she was still held in Alain's arms.

Eventually he carried her to a settee in the little parlour nearby, and stayed with her while she poured out the whole story.

'But why, why Marie-Rose?' she asked.

'I can't tell you that.' Alain still had his arm around her. 'It's the question we always ask. I've asked it myself when some of my men have fallen beside me. Why them and not me? There is no answer I can give you. When it is our time to go, we obey the summons. Marie-Rose was called tonight. She went quickly, be glad of that.'

Yvette gave a long shuddering sigh. 'Not quickly enough.'

'Remember her as she was,' he advised. 'That will be kindest to her. She was your friend, but she's gone.'

Yvette sighed again. The shock and horror had begun to recede a little, just talking to him.

There was a candle burning on the little table beside them. Yvette could not remember how it had got there or who had lit it. Perhaps Sister Marie had come in with it. By its light, she looked at Alain Renaud. He looked tired but well.

'Tell me about her,' he suggested now. 'You'll feel better if you talk about it.'

Yvette frowned and thought a moment. 'Marie-Rose was the youngest of us. She was only sixteen and so sweet tempered. Though she was a quiet little thing, she was always pleasant and cheerful.' She paused. 'She told me once she had an elder sister—and three brothers—yes, I'm sure it was three. I envied her for that. It was her sister who wanted her to come here because there was no dowry for her at home. If she had only known . . .' Yvette blew her nose angrily.

'She couldn't know,' Alain pointed out. 'She acted with the best intentions.'

A tear slid down Yvette's cheek. 'When I broke my leg, Marie-Rose made me a doll out of a clothes-peg and bits of material she begged from the others. She painted a face on it and found some yellow wool for curls.' She stole a look at Alain—he wasn't laughing at her, just nodding as though he understood. 'I was too old for dolls but it just fitted into my hand and I held it. It made me smile when the pain was bad.'

'She was kind.' The Captain was matter of fact. 'You'll always remember that and will pass her kindness on to someone else and think of her.'

'Yes,' Yvette agreed. 'I still have that peg doll—it's just a bit of wood. I'll show it to you some time.' She managed a watery smile. 'I think I kept it because no one had given me a present since my mother died.'

'How long ago was that?' Alain asked, his arm still around her waist. His hold was comfortable and comforting.

'Last year,' Yvette hesitated, trying to put her

thoughts together. 'It's not like France here in Montréal, is it—where decent folk can expect to sleep the night without danger?'

'No,' he seemed to understand her. 'Some things are better here. Your friend came for the chance of a home and family of her own. I'm very sorry we weren't in time to save her. We came in in the canoes from the river and we were singing and watching the stars as we paddled home, glad to be back with no casualties.' Alain was speaking softly.

Yvette was ashamed that he should think she blamed him. She murmured an apology and looked up at him. 'Was it hard—your mission? I never asked.'

Alain went on as though he had not heard her. 'It was so peaceful. Then we saw the smoke and beached our boats and left them, running. A burning house is always cause for alarm here . . . We killed two of the Indians but two got away.'

'Didn't you go after them?' Yvette hesitated to query that.

He shrugged. 'There's no use chasing Indians in the forest—that's an invitation to death. The fire was in the barn. We couldn't put that out but we saved the cow—and the house.'

'But won't they come back?'—Yvette's breath caught in her throat. 'The ones who got away, I mean.'

'Most unlikely,' the Captain's reply was firm.

Yvette was suddenly conscious that the candle on the table was burning low. It must be very late.

'Were any of your men hurt?' she asked, and couldn't help a yawn.

'Just the one you saw,' Alain replied. 'He had an arrow-wound, painful but not too serious.' He kissed her lightly on the forehead as one might do with a tired child. 'We'll go to the kitchen,' he suggested, 'and make ourselves and the good nuns a hot drink.' He handed her her crutches from the floor and picked up the stub of candle. Nursing the flame, he led her tap-tapping along the dark corridor. 'I have some of my tea ration left.' He drew a small pouch from his pocket. There was a pan of water boiling on the fire in the open hearth that was never allowed to go out. He measured tea into a medium-sized pot which Yvette found for him and ladled water onto it. The moon riding low in the sky shone wanly through the window over the sink.

It was so quiet they whispered. 'Milk? Cups?' he questioned, and the girl, glad of the warm glow cast by the fire, searched for them. She reached down two pewter mugs from their hooks and poured the steaming liquid into them. She wouldn't have believed it possible that she could feel so at home, so natural, with Alain Renaud in this hour before the dawn, alone and sorrow shared.

They sat in the most ordinary of wooden kitchen chairs at the scrubbed table, and presently Sister Jeanne and Sister Marie came in to join them.

'Sit down, Sisters,' said Alain, springing to his feet to serve them. 'It's been a terrible night for you.'

'For all of us,' said Sister Jeanne. 'But especially for that poor boy, Guillaume, and for Janine, who doesn't know yet her man is dead.'

'Janine?' Yvette licked dry lips. 'Was it her husband who went fishing with Guillaume and who died?'

Sister Jeanne looked at her, pity in her eyes. 'I thought you knew, child.'

Alain put his hand on Yvette's shoulder and poured her another cup of tea. 'Settlers—and their wives—must all be brave,' was all he said. Yvette had no more tears left. She looked up at him and put her hand on his and that touch calmed her.

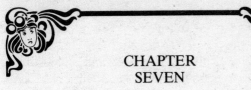

CHAPTER
SEVEN

EVERYONE turned out for the funeral of the three victims, from the governor himself down to the smallest child. Francine, wrapped in Yvette's shawl, accompanied her mother. It was a very pale Janine but she maintained a calm dignity as she sat nursing her baby—Georges's daughter whom he would never know. She sat in the front row with the governor, and Guillaume, mourning both his brother and his sister-in-law, was in the matching pew on the other side. Daniel and Marc were either side of him.

Yvette was in the second row with Pauline and Liliane as Marie-Rose's closest friends, and it was Pauline who held Yvette's hand.

Captain Renaud accompanied Sister Jeanne and Sister Marie in the pew behind.

After the long service they all followed in procession to the graveyard at the back of the church. The three pine boxes were lowered into holes in the dark earth, and they prayed.

'Ashes to ashes, dust to dust,' the priest intoned, 'in sure and certain knowledge of the life to come,' in the same measured tones that the *curé* had used at her mother's funeral, and Yvette tried to find some comfort in the ancient words. 'Man that is born of woman has but a short time to live. Jesus said I am the resurrection and the life; he that believeth in me, though he were dead, yet shall he live. Whosoever believeth in me shall never die.' The scent of incense was strong in the warm September morning as the altar-boys swung the censers again and earth was scattered on those bare boxes.

Guillaume threw a pretty nosegay of wild flowers on to the smallest coffin, his last tribute to Marie-Rose, the little girl who had been his brother's wife for two weeks only. Then it was over.

Yvette clung to Pauline, and Liliane wiped tears from her red-rimmed eyes. They huddled together, closer now than they had ever been—friends for ever, as Pauline declared.

So it was with the others in the congregation: all drawn into small groups, needing and finding reassurance in that contact with their neighbours.

Quietly, they dispersed. Yvette and Janine went back to the hospital with the nuns in a carriage.

It was two days after the funeral before life began to resume its normal pattern for Yvette. It wasn't that she forgot her friend but rather that life called out more strongly to be lived because of Marie-Rose. Life after all might not be long, but short.

It started again on the veranda, the veranda where she and Madame Brun-Cartier held court every afternoon. Yvette as usual was sewing.

Paul and Liliane brought their friend Albert

Pinault to call. Where Paul was dark, Albert was fair, but equally good looking. Yvette, in spite of warnings about *coureurs de bois*, was drawn to him. He told her she was a beautiful girl and asked her if she'd like to go canoeing on the river.

Yvette was charmed with the idea. 'Do you mean now?'

'Why not?' he smiled at her. 'I could carry you down and carry you back. You're just a slender slip of a girl, but all woman, I can clearly see.'

'Thank you,' the girl replied, flattered and pleased by his compliments. 'I'd love to. It would be cool on the river and peaceful. We could skim along like the Indians do and just enjoy ourselves.'

'Alone on the river with a lovely girl!' exclaimed Albert. 'What a delightful way to while away an afternoon. I could show you where the beavers build their dams and the wild ducks gather.'

'It sounds grand,' sighed Yvette. 'If only I could.'

'If only you could what?' asked another voice and Captain Renaud walked round the corner of the veranda.

'Canoe on the river,' said Albert, giving the Captain a mock salute.

'I hope you wouldn't do anything so foolish at this time,' Alain frowned.

'Nonsense,' Albert replied, 'there's very little danger on the river. One can see anything approaching.' He was very confident.

'Possibly.' Alain didn't want to argue. 'A man on his own wouldn't have any trouble, but it might be a different story with a crippled girl along.'

Yvette was indignant to hear herself referred to as that. She felt the eyes Albert turned on her held a different look. He had seen her as a girl before—a desirable girl—but the Captain's comment had changed that. Why did he spoil things for her?

Now Alain was talking to him. 'You've been among the Cat people, is there unrest there?'

Albert shrugged. 'They seemed peaceful enough, no menace there.'

'Let's forget Indians,' Paul broke in on the other two, 'there's been enough gloom and trouble. It was just an isolated incident. They happen and life goes on. That's what I keep telling Liliane but she's still all worked up about it. Tell me,' he turned towards Yvette, 'when will the splints come off your leg?'

'Sister Jeanne says next week or the week after,' she was pleased to tell him.

'We must make an occasion of it,' Albert was smiling at her. 'Paul shall bring his flute and Daniel his fiddle and I shall have the first dance.'

'That's if the Captain allows it,' Paul remarked slyly. 'I understand he regards himself as being in charge of Mademoiselle.'

'Do I?' asked Alain. 'Yes, perhaps so—I want to see no harm befalls this little bride.'

Yvette found herself blushing as they all looked at her.

'Anyone who wanted to marry her would have to ask your permission, then,' Albert winked at her.

Alain parried that. 'That's putting it a bit

strongly, but yes, I suppose my consent would be necessary.'

'What sort of man will you surrender her to?' asked Albert, his eyes still on Yvette.

This was too much for the girl. 'Do you intend to choose a husband for me, Captain?' she asked angrily. 'Why can't I choose for myself? All the others did.'

Captain Renaud's dark eyes met hers. 'If you have any preference you have only to tell me. I'm not an unreasonable man.'

Paul began to laugh. 'You're not a married man either.'

'What do you mean by that?' Captain Renaud's eyebrows rose in interrogation.

Madame Brun-Cartier had been following this exchange with some amusement. 'I think Paul means you are more accustomed to managing men than women,' she observed dryly.

'I shall choose for myself.' Yvette stabbed her needle into the unoffending dress she was working on as though to emphasise her point.

'We'll see.' Alain Renaud patted her head.

Madame Brun-Cartier gave a cackle of laughter. 'I shall observe that with interest and act as go-between when your tempers rise.'

Yvette would have liked to have gathered her sewing together and swept away from all of them but there was no way a girl on crutches could make that kind of dramatic exit, so she contented herself with determining that she would choose her own man, absolutely, finally, and without consulting Captain Renaud. However good he had been to her the other night he had no right to dictate to her about the man she married.

Paul and Liliane and Albert left soon after that and then Alain disappeared to visit the soldier who had been injured and left in the hospital the night he had returned.

'Liked that Albert, didn't you?' Madame asked. 'I told you he was quite a man. Whatever Captain Renaud says, a man who made up his mind to it could win you. Where's Marc these days?'

'Busy, I suppose,' Yvette replied, but she had been wondering the same thing herself. Did she imagine it or had Alain been warning her in some way about Marc by saying she would need his permission?

As it happened, Marc visited her the next day and so did Nicholas from the brewery. Marc brought sheets from the governor's wife for the hospital and Nicholas brought eels.

Alain joined them on the veranda for a while and did his best to hold a conversation with the brewer, but had no better luck than Yvette with that silent man.

'Do you suppose a drink of his own ale would loosen his tongue?' the irrepressible Marc whispered to the girl, and she couldn't stop giggling in spite of Alain's disapproving eyes upon her.

Then Marc compounded the situation by asking Madame Brun-Cartier in a loud whisper if she would favour his suit and put in a good word for him with the Captain.

Madame replied that she favoured Albert, who had come the day before, and Marc was taken aback.

'I thought you liked me,' he protested.

'What has liking to do with it?' she demanded. 'You're too practised.'

Whether that went home or not Yvette couldn't decide, but Marc made the old lady laugh by adopting a mournful expression and begging her to change her mind.

When Nicholas pushed his chair closer to Yvette's, Alain called Marc aside and, try as she would, she could not hear what they said to each other but they both looked serious and both left, Marc kissing Yvette's hand and Madame Brun-Cartier's, Alain merely waving to them and saying he had business to attend to. Why did he always interfere when interesting men came to see her?

Nicholas stayed for some time, but he was as quiet as ever. Yvette sewed on while Madame tried to encourage him into expressing an opinion on whether the fine weather would continue.

When he finally left, Sister Jeanne called Yvette into her little office.

The girl was surprised, not quite sure if the nun was displeased by the number of visitors on the veranda. She motioned Yvette to a seat and said she had been giving some thought to her future.

'When the splints are taken off your leg,' she told

her, 'I don't want you to feel that you are no longer welcome here. You will need a little time for your leg to lose its stiffness and return to normal.' She smiled kindly. 'There should be no need for you to go through the ordeal of the Choosing as the other girls who came with you did. I'm sure your future will be secure. I'm pleased so many good men have been turning their attention to helping the hospital.' There was a sparkle in her eyes and an answering smile from Yvette at this way of acknowledging Yvette's suitors.

'I'm sure, with Captain Renaud's help,' Sister Jeanne continued, 'you need have no fear of an unhappy match. He'll see you're properly provided for.'

Yvette frowned at that. She was determined the choice of which man she accepted was going to be hers, not Alain's, but she bit her lip and listened. There was no sense in antagonising Sister Jeanne.

'I don't know whether Captain Renaud has told you about Marie-Rose's brother-in-law. Young Guillaume came to see the Captain and offered for you. It would be a very suitable marriage. He owns the farm now and with Marie-Rose's dowry—and yours of course—it would be quite a respectable holding. Guillaume is a nice lad, too, and a good worker.' Sister Jeanne paused as though to allow Yvette time to digest this information and appeared to be waiting for some kind of comment.

Yvette felt a little breathless. She hadn't really expected this. Sister Jeanne was right. Guillaume was a nice lad but he seemed scarcely old enough for a husband.

'I had no idea,' she stammered. Suddenly, it was all happening too quickly.

Sister Jeanne was understanding. 'Captain Renaud was as surprised as you, I think.' Her tone was dry. 'He advised Guillaume not to rush into any decisions until his grief and shock had lessened. In any case, he pointed out you weren't ready or fit.'

Yvette gulped. Conflicting emotions shook her—gratitude to Alain for preventing any hasty action, pity for Guillaume, and a decided disinclination to make any final decisions yet. What was wrong with her? Here was a heaven-sent opportunity to assert herself and make up her mind to accept a man she liked and felt in sympathy with. Yet she felt grateful to the Captain for having put off the necessity of saying yes or no. She couldn't understand herself.

'I think it likely there'll be other offers,' Sister Jeanne phrased it delicately. 'If you have any strong preferences you have only to speak to Captain Renaud—or indeed to me if you feel more at ease with me.' She put up her hand as Yvette's mouth opened. 'No, no don't say anything now. Think about what I've said. You can talk to me any time.'

Yvette thanked the good sister and promised that she would. She went away in a thoughtful mood. It was good to have a friend who exerted no pressure on her and promised her a roof over her head. Well, what did she want or rather whom did she want? Yvette asked herself that question and couldn't bring herself to answer it. She saw Marc's laughing eyes, and Daniel's shrewd ones, even Guillaume's sad ones and always in her mind's eye, the Captain's. The question swept from the back of her mind—'and what if my leg does not heal properly?' Better not to think about any of it. She pushed the whole subject of the future firmly away, and told herself to concentrate on the present.

It was the Captain himself who forced her to think of what was to become of her. One morning Sister Marie told her he was in Sister Jeanne's little office and wanted to see her.

Yvette was unaccountably nervous as she entered the room. Her crutches squeaked against the floor as she lowered herself into the wicker chair he indicated from his position at the desk. So this was to be a formal interview. She waited for him to speak, but he was writing.

A beam of sunshine struggled through the lace curtains where they were gently lifted by a stray breeze and fell in tiny particles upon his cheek. Yvette noted the squareness of his jaw-line, the golden brown of his complexion and reflected that there was something very pleasing about his whole appearance, not as good-looking as Marc, nor as rugged as Daniel, but still . . . he was very masculine.

He seemed in no hurry to break the quiet, disturbed only by the scratch of his racing pen. Yvette, instead of being nonplussed by this, began to relax. She had never found him an easy man or even a comfortable one to be with, but to her surprise as she watched the speckled sunshine drift across his countenance she settled into her chair, the tension gone from her arms and legs.

He smiled at her and her heart melted within her. He was going to be kind, as he had been the night of Marie-Rose's death. She smiled in return.

'I have something for you,' he began.

She lifted enquiring eyes. 'For me?'

'Your leg will soon be healed and I have brought you some moccasins. At first I thought to keep them till you had thrown away your crutches, but then I asked myself why not give you the pleasure now of receiving a gift?' He produced a small leather bag and rose to his feet and approached her with it. Instead of giving it to her, he stood above her for a moment. 'I understand you know of Guillaume's offer.'

Yvette nodded. She didn't want to talk of that. She wanted to see the moccasins.

Perhaps he sensed that, for he began to speak again.

'May they smooth your path, may they soften your way and keep your feet warm and safe from thorns and sharp stones.' He handed it to her. 'That's what the Indians say,' he smiled charmingly. 'They have a gift for flowery rhetoric which seems to have rubbed off on me.'

He remained standing beside her.

Yvette pulled at the thongs that sealed the bag and took out the moccasins. They were soft tan leather, beaded and fringed, much prettier than the pair she had refused to buy on *Le Poisson Bleu*.

'How kind of you,' she exclaimed, colouring with pleasure.

'It's nothing really,' he protested. 'When one visits with the Indians one both gives and receives presents. It is the custom. When these were given to me I thought of you. Go ahead, try one on.'

Yvette did as she was bid. She quickly unlaced the old soft slipper shoe she wore on her good foot and tried the moccasin. It slipped on neatly, fitting as though it had been made for her.

'It's perfect,' she said and looked up at him, an imp of mischief in her eyes. 'What sort of gifts did you bring to the Indians?'

He leaned on the edge of the table, half sitting there. 'Some beads, a cooking-pot, knives, a silver bracelet. They would have preferred muskets or brandy.'

Yvette might have questioned him about the guns or alcohol but her mind registered 'silver bracelet'. So it had not been for the fair Hélène in Québec. She smiled happily at him and if he wondered why she smiled she didn't care. Suddenly she was extraordinarily pleased with life and with the Captain's present. Her hand lingered on the moccasin she still held in her lap, tracing the patterned beads.

'If these beads are money to them, why do they use them as decoration?' she asked.

Alain shrugged, 'To show their wealth, to impress the recipient with the esteem in which they hold him.'

A warm glow spread through Yvette at his words. If the esteem was true of the Indians, did that mean it was true for her? He had said that he had thought of her immediately he had been given them. It was foolish to leap to conclusions because he had thought of her, but she felt like singing or dancing.

His next words served to confirm this feeling.

'I'm pleased with you,' he announced. 'I hear good things of you. Sister Marie tells me you have a real talent with the babies and you've made friends with their mothers too.'

Yvette basked in the sunlight of his approval. 'They are very kind to me here,' she murmured, and thought how nice he could be when he tried— not like he had been in the closed carriage. And yet, and yet . . . her heart beat faster at that memory. Today he had not touched her.

She was drawn back to the present by his next words.

'I'm delighted,' he went on, 'as you must be, by the numbers and quality of the men who are calling to see you.'

That was strange, she told herself. On the veranda he never seemed delighted but rather disagreeable and omnipresent.

'I thought a word of warning, of caution, rather,' he amended, 'might be in order. You know, Yvette, that I have your best interests at heart.'

Yvette nodded, not quite sure where he was leading. After the comfort he had given on the night of Marie-Rose's death, she could not doubt it.

'I have received several other requests for permission to pay court to you.' His voice was even. 'I have considered them all with great care, and I have decided . . .' He paused.

The dream-like quality of the occasion was shattered for the girl. It was the confidence of his voice when he said, 'I have decided.'

Yvette sat erect. The sheer conceit of the man to decide her life for her—she could not accept it. She stopped him in mid-sentence. 'If I had been permitted to take part in the Choosing,' she exclaimed, 'I would have done the deciding, would I not?'

'Yes,' he admitted, 'that is so, but the situation is different now.'

'How different?' The girl's anger was apparent in the redness of her cheeks.

'I am here to help you, to guide you a little, to steer you away from mistakes.' The Captain might have been explaining to a child. 'Let me finish what I was going to say.'

Yvette opened her mouth but shut it again, trying to hold back her temper as he went on.

'I want you to know my views about the most suitable men.' He hesitated. '*Coureurs de bois* do not make the most faithful of husbands,' he pointed out, 'and smooth tongues are not always to be trusted.'

Yvette's good foot tapped against the floor. 'Do you mean Marc?' she asked coldly.

'Marc—and others,' he agreed.

'Let's start with Marc,' she suggested. 'Is that the only fault you find with him? A smooth tongue?'

'I don't think his attentions are serious.' The Captain's relaxed leaning on the desk was gone. He was on his feet above her.

'How can you know that?' Yvette enquired. 'He's not married, is he?'

Alain shook his head. 'No.'

'Has he said he will not marry?' she asked.

'Not in so many words.'

'You've guessed, perhaps?' Yvette's tone was honeyed.

The Captain shrugged. 'Take my word for it,' he suggested.

'If he did ask,' she prompted, 'would I be free to accept him?'

'Yes, of course.' His reply was stiff.

They glared at each other. Yvette would not give in. She would decide her husband herself. She must make that clear to him. When he was friendly to her she liked him a good deal, but why did he interfere?

'I came to this new land of hardship and danger and independence,' she told him raggedly but with increasing confidence, 'to choose for myself—and I intend to do just that. When I am asked by Marc, I shall know how to reply.'

She could see that did not please him.

'I have no more to say, then,' he told her coldly. 'If you do not want my help I have no intention of forcing it upon you. You may go—but remember I shall not stand by and allow you to marry someone wholly unsuitable.' He handed her her crutches. 'Think well on that.'

'I shall,' she told him, 'and I thank you for the moccasins—if not for the advice.'

Yvette rose to her feet. She resented this power over her which he had accorded to himself. She stuffed the moccasin and the slipper into the leather bag without even thinking of what she was doing. Whatever he said, she would choose her own husband and he would in the end have to accept that. She hopped from the room without another word. She would not allow him to arrange her life for her. Why did he make her fight him? If he had been her friend . . .

In the next few days there seemed to Yvette a different pace to life, more earnest, more devious, somehow quickened. Where before she had looked forward to the afternoons as a social time, a time for enjoyment, now they were a testing time—testing against the Captain's words and in his absence, for he did not come. Was he letting her go her own way or just busy with his duties? She began to study the men who visited and to consider what each would be like as a husband. She refused to admit to herself that she missed the fair officer.

The first to come under this searching scrutiny

was Daniel, the saw-mill manager. He arrived the next afternoon.

Yvette looked up from her sewing, and there he was with a nanny-goat on a string approaching along the side path.

Daniel waved to her and the goat either took fright at something in the bushes or realised his attention was momentarily diverted and took the opportunity to bolt.

With a squeal of triumph she disappeared into the trees beyond the path and Daniel went in hot pursuit.

There was a great crashing in the undergrowth. The goat bleated and he shouted. Madame Brun-Cartier's harsh laugh cackled as she offered advice.

Yvette giggled till the tears ran down her face, then she picked up her crutches and hopped outside to the path.

Daniel was still calling to the animal and becoming more and more impatient. The goat was leading him in circles by the sound of it, slipping from his grasp every time he got near her.

There was a fearful crash. Daniel must have tripped and fallen. He groaned and then shouted, *'Diable, cochon.'*

She reflected that he must be thoroughly exasperated to be calling the poor animal first a devil, then a pig, but it said a good deal for the evenness of his temperament that he used no stronger language than that.

As Yvette stood there, the goat's head appeared

in the bushes chewing at a branch. Daintily she flicked a leaf into her mouth and then another as the girl watched her.

'*Vien'ci*, come here, nanny', called Yvette softly, making a clicking noise with her tongue and the goat took a step closer.

The girl stood still, afraid to move because the crutches might alarm the animal. There was no sound from Daniel. Either he had completely lost the track and moved further away or he was creeping up to them noiselessly.

Yvette called again and the animal ambled forward, contentedly rubbing her head against Yvette's leg and nearly knocking her over. She just managed to keep her balance and to grasp the cord that dangled from the nanny's neck.

To Yvette's relief, Sister Marie came and led the animal to the cowshed as the discomfited Daniel walked out of the bushes.

'I think that goat prefers women to men,' he said ruefully. 'Look how gentle and obedient she is now. They told me she was so nice natured a child could handle her, but I've had a terrible time.' He brushed leaves and dirt from his clothes.

'Come and sit down,' suggested Yvette, leading him towards the veranda, 'and tell us why you've brought a goat here.' Her shoulders were shaking with laughter.

'Go ahead, laugh,' he exclaimed, smiling himself. 'No man wants to look a fool, but if you are you might as well admit it.' He sank into a chair.

Yvette laughed out loud and Madame Brun-Cartier joined in.

'You looked so funny', she declared, but she liked the way he was taking it. 'I'm sorry, Daniel, if you could just have seen yourself.' She giggled again.

Madame Brun-Cartier had herself in better control now. 'Whose goat is it,' she asked, 'and why is she here?'

'She's here because I brought her,' Daniel replied.

With that reply Yvette had great difficulty in maintaining a straight face.

'I borrowed her from Madame Napier. She said goat's milk was good for babies. It's for Francine.' Daniel paused. 'One of my neighbours came to visit Janine yesterday and she said her milk had dried up and the baby was hungry. I was brought up on goat's milk so I know it's good and I knew Madame Napier had fed her baby with goat's milk.'

'You're a really kind man.' Yvette was regretting the way she had laughed at him in the bushes. 'We must tell Sister Marie and Janine the good news.'

Yvette was surprised to see that Daniel and Janine greeted each other as old friends. Daniel said Janine lived near the saw-mill and they talked about all the new homesteads in that area. It seemed to Yvette that the other girl liked Daniel. Well why shouldn't she, she asked herself. He was a good man and would make a good husband. It was perhaps as Madame said—things changed. A girl became a widow and she was eligible to remarry.

A thoughtful Yvette went to bed that night pondering about men and husbands. What sort of husband would Marc make, she wondered. He was easy to talk to, pleasant to be with, and she liked him—but Alain Renaud had said he would never marry her.

A small voice inside her questioned what the Captain would be like as a husband. She tried to banish that thought. 'Horrid,' she told herself, 'overbearing, set on his own way,' and then she remembered his gentleness the night her friend had died and she sighed and told herself he was a soldier, not a suitor—and fell asleep.

In the morning, the baby Francine eagerly took the goat's milk as she had done the evening before, and her mother smiled and laughed with Yvette for the first time since her husband's death.

Yvette looked up from this pleasant exchange to see Pauline beckoning to her from the doorway. She went to her.

'I must talk to you,' urged Pauline. 'Can we be private?'

Yvette led her into the little parlour and they sat down facing each other in two hard-backed chairs.

'It's about Liliane,' Pauline began. 'Her husband has gone.'

'Paul gone?' echoed Yvette. 'Gone where?'

'To the bush—the forest—the Indians,' Pauline shuddered. 'He's turned *coureur de bois*. It's that friend of his, that Albert, and his brother who are responsible. They turned his head with talk of the profits they'll make in the fur trade. Get-rich-quick ideas are fine for single men, but where's the sense of it for a married man?' Pauline paused for breath.

'How's Liliane taking it?' Yvette managed to slide a question in.

'Screaming and carrying on,' responded Pauline. She came to see me two nights ago. I had to take her upstairs she was making so much noise, and it upset the customers in the shop. Pierre didn't like it at all.

'How will she live?' asked Yvette, trying to be practical and not drawn into a discussion of Monsieur Michelin's feelings. 'What will she do?'

'That's what I've come to see you about.' Pauline put her hand on Yvette's. 'She doesn't know what to do with herself. She came into the shop yesterday morning again—in fact she went to all the shops yesterday.' She hesitated. 'I don't know how to put this.' Once again she stopped.

Yvette looked at her. Pauline's hand was trembling and she was biting her lip. Her own hand closed over Pauline's and the other girl seemingly took courage from that.

'She's taken things from the shop—from all the shops—just little things mostly—stolen them,' Pauline whispered the last phrase. 'Two of the shop people came and told me. They were sorry for her, but they won't go on being sorry for her as their stock disappears. I spoke to Liliane and she won't listen to me. She says they're lying. What can I do?' Pauline's arms opened in a gesture that was almost supplication. 'If she goes on like this you know what will happen. She'll be arrested and beaten, maybe sent back to France. She must be stopped. She'll be whipped through the streets or put in the stocks,' Pauline gulped. There were tears in her eyes. 'Pierre says it will only be what she deserves if she's caught. Tell me, that day with the combs— would she have taken them?'

'I don't know.' Yvette had wondered that herself. 'I know she's not a wicked girl, just weak and silly. Do you think there's any way of saving her?' She was worried. Liliane seemed bent on self-destruction.

Pauline had an air of determination about her. 'There's only one way,' she announced. 'She must be thoroughly frightened.'

'Frightened?' Yvette protested. 'Now? When she's already upset about Paul's going. How can you even think of it?'

'It's the idea of Madame Leger in the chocolate shop,' Pauline explained. 'She's a wise old lady. Oh, I know it sounds cruel—but it's being cruel to be kind. It's better to be frightened than to be beaten with everyone in the town watching.'

Yvette nodded slowly. 'I can see you have an idea how it could be done. Tell me.'

'Madame Leger is willing to have it happen in her shop,' Pauline began, 'but we'll need your help. She says everyone pinches chocolates from her.'

Yvette was puzzled by this. Where did she come into it, she wanted to know.

'It's Captain Renaud, of course,' Pauline told

her. 'He must be there when she's caught. If you'll speak to the Captain and arrange it with him. He'll listen to you.'

'Why Captain Renaud?' Yvette was beginning to see the sense of the plan.

'For some reason she's very much in awe of him,' Pauline spoke slowly. 'I know because she's told me. If you could explain it to him and ask him to threaten her firmly with deportation she'd listen to him—and he wouldn't have to report it to anyone. You'd get him to promise that.'

Yvette didn't like any of this. She was sure Captain Renaud would not want to take part in this scheme. She tried to dissuade Pauline, but the other girl proved unexpectedly obdurate and convinced it was the only way of saving Liliane.

Yvette suggested Pierre might speak to her or Sister Jeanne, perhaps, but Pauline was absolutely sure neither of them would be official enough to make an impression on Liliane.

Eventually and very unwillingly Yvette gave way and agreed to ask the Captain that very afternoon, if he should happen to come. She couldn't explain her reluctance even to herself, and certainly not to Pauline, who kept insisting that the Captain would listen to her and be sure to do as she asked. She promised to do her best with a heavy heart. She had saved Liliane's life once; she must try again.

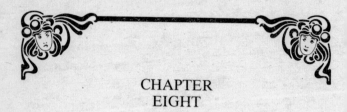

CHAPTER
EIGHT

YVETTE knew she would have to see Captain Renaud on his own. She didn't want Madame Brun-Cartier listening. She thought and puzzled about how this could be managed. She was very well aware that Madame acted as chaperon and satisfied all the conventions about a single girl never being alone with a man. Strange, the only man she had ever been alone with in Ville-Marie for any length of time was the Captain, and those encounters had been entirely unsought on her part. Now, she must seek him out. What would he think?

She was sure he wouldn't want to be involved in this scheme of Pauline's—and she didn't want him involved with Liliane in any case. Liliane was too pretty, too dependent, too appealing. Liliane without a husband—she put the thought out of her mind. She had promised Pauline and she was honestly upset about Liliane. What was the matter with her? Just because she had parted from the Captain in anger, and he hadn't spoken to her since, she was allowing herself to make excuses about seeking him out. She must ask his help. There was no escaping that.

Finally she decided the only thing she could do was to pass Alain a note when he called that afternoon and let him manage the situation. If he made the first move no one would question him or comment about it. Madame Brun-Cartier's curiosity and interest would not be aroused.

Accordingly, when they were settled on the veranda, Yvette dropped a piece of her sewing at Alain's feet.

He picked it up and she gave him a slip of paper on which she had written, 'Please, invent some excuse, I want to be alone with you.'

She watched him as he read it keeping it in the palm of his hand. Only a slight twitch of his eyebrows revealed his surprise.

Madame Brun-Cartier was regaling him with the story of the goat's arrival, and at the end of it Alain pushed his chair back and held out his hand to the girl.

'Where is this animal? In the cowshed? Come, you shall show me.'

Yvette led the way along the side of the building to the shed.

Once out of range of Madame Brun-Cartier's vision he halted, leaning against a tree.

'Now then,' he demanded, 'what's happened that you must write to me and be alone with me? Has someone proposed?' There was a half smile on his lips. 'Sit beside me.' He indicated a wooden bench a little distance away. He helped her over the rough ground and they sat down together. 'We're friends today, are we?' he smiled at her.

It occurred to Yvette that it would have been very pleasant to sit there with him and be friends, but she drew away a little and began to speak.

'It's about Liliane,' she blurted out.

'What about Liliane?' he asked. 'I know her husband's gone to the woods. There's nothing you or I can do about that.' He put his hand on one of Yvette's curls which fell over her shoulder and rested on his since he was sitting so close to her. He pulled it gently and then released it so that it sprang back into place. 'You have lovely hair,' he murmured.

It was quiet and peaceful in this back garden. A red and orange butterfly flew over a bush and Yvette could see small white ones fluttering over the cabbages only a few metres away. The sun was warm on her face and Captain Renaud was very near and in a very soft mood. A lazy sort of contentment stole over her. When he took her hand in his, her heart began to beat faster.

This would never do. She had come to talk about Liliane—and talk she must. 'Liliane has been taking things from the shops and Pauline says we must stop her,' she said baldly.

'We?' the Captain asked coldly. He dropped her hand. 'What is that supposed to mean—is she in some sort of trouble? I don't want anything to do with it.'

Yvette bit her lip. This was every bit as bad as she had feared. 'You must frighten her.' She looked into his eyes and withdrew along the bench at their expression.

'You needn't draw back from me,' he exclaimed. 'I'm not going to bite you—or shake you—though I'd dearly like to. You'd best explain.'

Yvette knew she had handled it ineptly and it made her nervous and tongue-tied, but she managed to give him a coherent story with only a few pauses for breath.

'Can you? Will you?' She was frightened to ask, but she forced herself for Liliane's sake, in spite of the closed look on his face. 'Pauline thinks if she were really frightened enough, Liliane would stop doing it.'

'And I'm the one to do that, am I? Put the fear of God and earthly punishment into her—am I? Well, answer me . . .' He began to shake her. 'Is that how you see me—a man to frighten young girls? Look at me and tell me honestly, do I scare you?'

Yvette looked into those dark eyes so close to her own. She felt only the truth would do now. 'Sometimes,' she whispered and looked down at her hands.

She felt her chin taken in a firm grasp and she was forced to meet his eyes again, much closer now.

'Were you frightened of me the other night when I held you in my arms?'

Yvette shook her head, disturbed by his nearness. She couldn't tell him how safe, how protected, she had felt that night, how he had comforted her.

But he was not going to let her remain silent. 'How did you feel?' he asked softly.

Her heart was hammering a message against her breast. How could he not hear it? She was lost in his gaze, drowned in the depths of his blazing eyes. Heaven help her, she wanted to remain there, captive, enthralled. But he was willing her to give an honest answer.

'As though—as though I'd come home,' she murmured. 'I never knew my father, but I think he might have been like you were then. I understood why your men love you. I know they do,' she added, as the expression on his face changed to surprise. 'I've talked to your man who's still in hospital here with his wound. He says a good officer is part leader and part father.'

Alain kissed her gently on the mouth and for a sweet moment her lips clung to his.

'Love is a strong word,' he declared, his hand holding hers again. 'It was a nice thing to say. So that's the way you see yourself—as one of my men—I suppose I've brought that on myself by telling you you were.'

'I don't, I'm not,' Yvette protested shakily, her senses still trembling from the taste of his kiss. What did he want of her? She longed to have his arms around her again. 'Liliane needs your help,' she whispered. 'You helped me the other night.'

'Yes,' he agreed, 'but you are different.' He rose to his feet. He did not explain how she was different or why. Yvette was left wondering about that.

Captain Renaud began to pace up and down.

Yvette said nothing—just watched him.

He halted abruptly in front of her. 'This Liliane is an empty-headed creature—but she's your friend. I'm glad to see you're loyal to your friends.'

Yvette began to hope at that, but his next words didn't please her much.

'She's a pretty little thing,' he went on musingly. 'It would be a pity to see her whipped through the town . . . and sent back to France . . . but she must change her ways.'

'You'll do it, then?' Yvette's voice shook. 'You'll speak to her?'

'*Peut-être.*' He frowned down at her, considering. 'It shouldn't be too hard to frighten her. After all if I can scare you who fight me every inch of the way, I should have no trouble terrifying Liliane, should I?'

'No.' Yvette wasn't sure how to reply, but he appeared to be waiting for an answer.

'You needn't have said that so quickly or so emphatically,' she was told with a glance of distaste.

'Will it do any good if she has nothing to fill her life?' Alain was remote, lost in his own thoughts. That moment of shared emotion when they kissed might never have happened, so far away did he seem now.

'I don't know.' Yvette brought her thoughts back to Liliane and her problems. 'What will she do with Paul away, perhaps gone forever?'

'What most women do,' Alain spoke without stopping for thought this time. 'Find comfort elsewhere.'

Yvette was embarrassed and angry. 'It won't be like that,' she assured him. 'Liliane will wait for Paul to return, however long it takes.'

'Oh yes, she'll mean to,' he replied coolly, 'but he'll be away for a considerable time.'

Yvette protested again, but again he cut her short. 'Remember I've seen it all before—you haven't,' he pointed out. 'There are too few women here, and too many men.' There was a brooding expression in his eyes. 'Liliane is a very pretty girl,' he paused, 'and she'll be lonely.'

Yvette's heart sank. She doubted that Liliane had enough resources within herself to stand a long absence on Paul's part. 'Men,' she exclaimed, a world of helplessness in her voice. 'Don't they ever think?' She continued almost to herself, 'Marc said Paul was a nearly man. I said he couldn't be nearly married—but I think he's proved me wrong.'

Alain gave her a sudden smile. 'Probably his intentions were the best in the world. He wants to make a fortune and shower Liliane with good things, but to my mind if a man takes a wife he should stay with her and give her his support.'

Yvette agreed with that wholeheartedly. 'If you married,' she asked hesitantly, 'and you were still a soldier, you might have to leave your wife.'

'If I were to think of marriage—which I am not

doing at the moment—I would leave the army.'
Alain's voice was very sure.

Yvette felt she had been firmly put in her place
but she refused to allow that. She persisted. 'Would
you ever leave the army willingly? Isn't it your
career?'

Alain gave her a long look, then he shrugged, 'I
have sometimes thought of settling in New France.
I've been here four years and I like the country. A
man could hope to make his mark here or, like
Paul, his fortune, but I like Québec better than
Montréal. It's more established, more sociable.'

So it was true then about this Hélène in Québec,
thought Yvette. He wanted to get back there. It
was nothing to her what he chose to do, where he
chose to go.

Abruptly she rose from the bench. 'Well, if you
wish to see the goat, you must open the door and go
in,' she indicated the shed.

'I shall forgo that pleasure,' he assured her. 'I
came only for the sake of your company.' He
bowed to her and held out his hand to steady her as
she swung back to the path.

Yvette felt the warmth of his fingers and a tingling sensation where his palm rested on her arm. Impatiently, she shook him off. She was shocked and
ashamed of the effect his touch aroused in her. It
was plain he might kiss her and put his arms around
her but he had told her he had no thought of
marriage. She burned with indignation.

If he had not agreed to speak to Liliane, she

would have berated him for kissing her, she told herself sternly. Instead, she said nothing and led the way back to the veranda. But she couldn't help wondering what he might have done next.

Alain soon took his departure, and though Madame Brun-Cartier had given her a very shrewd look when they returned, she had made no remarks about their absence.

Daniel came later that afternoon. He went in to visit Janine and Francine while he was there and came out well pleased with Francine's progress.

Then Marc arrived with sheets for the hospital from Madame Archambault. 'She doesn't want to be outdone by the governor's wife,' he told them, and made them both laugh at the droll way he spoke.

Yvette asked him to take a message to Pauline suggesting that she call again.

'I thought you weren't friends,' he teased her. 'Does she know about the combs?'

Yvette replied she did know, but somehow it no longer seemed important. She would have liked to talk to Marc about the business of Liliane because he often had good ideas, but she was aware that the fewer people who heard about that the better.

He had heard of course about Paul's turning *coureur de bois* and going off with Albert and Jean.

'When I heard that Albert was calling on you, dear girl,' Marc still had a twinkle in his eye, 'I thought you'd made a conquest. What did you say or do to send him off so quickly?'

Yvette protested that she had done nothing, and the subject of Liliane was forgotten.

But that night Yvette lay awake for a long time thinking about her and wondering how she was managing, and hoping they hadn't made things worse for her by interfering. It was strange that they'd all come to make a new worth-while life here, and in a few short weeks Marie-Rose and her husband were dead, Liliane in trouble and herself in hospital with a broken leg. That at least was healing—she was almost sure of that—and with the quantities of bear grease she'd applied and the Captain's faith in that—why of course it would be all right. She drifted off to troubled sleep in which Liliane pursued her, threatening her with her own crutches.

Yvette waited all through the next day for news but none came. No one visited. However, she put the finishing touches to Madame Archambault's dress and was well pleased with it. It was everything she had hoped and she felt reasonably sure that Madame would be pleased with it.

She expected Pauline, but the following morning it was Liliane who called on her, a smiling, excited, Liliane.

The surprised Yvette showed her into the small parlour and they sat down.

'It's what I've always wanted,' Liliane began. 'I'm going to start working tomorrow in Leger's chocolate shop. I shall be selling those lovely sweets and learning to make them. It's all arranged.'

'That's good news!' Yvette was delighted for her friend. 'How did this happen?'

'It's all due to Captain Renaud,' Liliane confided. 'Isn't he a wonderful man? He was so sympathetic about Paul going off into the woods with Albert and Jean. Of course Paul's going to make a lot of money but it does leave me on my own, doesn't it? Captain Renaud says I must be very brave and learn to manage on my own. That's what Paul would expect, after all.' Liliane rushed on with a bewildered Yvette wondering if the Captain had ever delivered his warning to this enthusiastic girl. But she said nothing. She couldn't stop the flow.

'Captain Renaud,' Liliane's smile was artlessly innocent. 'He said I could call him Alain if I wanted. Alain had heard that Madame Leger was looking for an assistant and he suggested me. He went with me when I went to see her and he was so forceful and masterful. She admitted that I was just the person to help her. Alain told her so. Wasn't that kind of him?'

Yvette agreed. But the unbidden, unwelcome thought of a grateful Liliane centring her affections on Alain surfaced in her mind.

'I'm going to work so hard to prove how right he was about me. Even when I was a little girl I wanted to have a shop, and one day when Madame Leger's older—and it stands to reason she can't live for ever—well, she is old and white-haired, isn't she?'

Liliane paused for breath and Yvette paused to unravel the ramifications of all this in her mind. 'When Paul comes back with the furs or the money I might be able to buy her out and have my very own shop.' Liliane sat back in complete satisfaction.

'I'm very pleased for you,' declared Yvette, 'but aren't you missing Paul?'

'Yes,' sighed Liliane, 'but I haven't known him very long, have I? And Alain says I must just get used to that. He says we're both working for the same purpose. Paul probably won't be gone all that long and you don't know what it's like to be married anyway and have to get all those big meals ready on time. Madame Leger will give me a hot meal every day and I can have chocolates whenever I want. You must come and visit me in the shop.'

Yvette agreed to do that when the splints were off her leg.

'I've got more good news,' Liliane continued. 'I've been invited to the Governor's Ball next week. Paul and I were both invited but Alain says it will be all right for me to go. There'll be extra men there for me to dance with—there always are—Alain is going himself and that nice Marc that we met on the ship—and quite a few soldiers.' She breathed in. 'Pauline and Pierre invited me to go with them, so that will be good too. Have you received an invitation?'

Yvette shook her head. She felt upset. This must be the same dance for which Madame Archambault had ordered the dress. Why were the others invited and not she? Because she didn't have a husband? How unfair that was when there were going to be unattached men there and they'd all be dancing with Liliane and paying her compliments. With her fair hair and the new becoming colour in her cheeks she was very pretty, and couldn't help but be popular with the men. Even if her leg was still in splints by then, she could sit and watch and enjoy it all. Yvette felt left out and neglected.

'I just didn't know what I could wear for it,' Liliane was prattling on, 'but my next-door neighbour offered to lend me a lovely blue dress. It just matches my eyes. I'll have to take it in a little at the waist, of course, but that's easily done. It's a beautiful dress. Alain said he'd take care of me so he's sure to ask me to dance, and Marc too. I am looking forward to it.'

Well she might, Yvette reflected, and if she's going to be eating chocolates all day long she'll soon be letting out the waist. Then she felt ashamed of herself and tried not to be jealous of her friend's good fortune. But it rankled that she had only herself to blame. She had asked Alain to speak to Liliane, who was a pretty girl temporarily without a husband and intent on making the most of that. The way she was peppering the conversation with 'Alain says' it was obvious that Alain had made a powerful impression and that she wanted him as a friend.

Yvette wrestled with her black thoughts and tried not to let them show. She couldn't help reflecting wryly that whereas she had saved Liliane's life and her reputation and had a broken leg to show for it, Liliane was sailing through life quite comfortably.

'Don't you feel well?' asked Liliane. 'You're so quiet. Is your leg hurting?' she asked looking so concerned that Yvette's heart melted. It was a poor friend who couldn't be glad about another's good fortune. She summoned a smile and said she was feeling fine—just tired in this hot weather.

Yvette fought with the strange sensations and feelings that were bothering her. Jealousy? No, it couldn't be jealousy, but she wanted to scratch and claw at this complacent girl. What did she mean when she declared that Alain had promised to look after her? What had she offered in return?

Liliane patted her hand solicitously. 'You're going to be all right. Everyone says it's very warm for nearly the end of September. You'll soon be able to throw away those crutches. How many weeks has it been?'

'About six now,' Yvette replied. 'Sister Jeanne says the splints will come off next week probably but I'd like to know what's happening now.'

'It's healing itself. I'm sure you're worrying about nothing.' Liliane dismissed the subject and took her leave.

A very thoughtful Yvette hopped to the door with Liliane and then went to prepare a bottle of goat's milk for the baby Francine.

'I shall be going home soon,' announced her

young mother Janine, 'now that baby's doing so
well. Will you come to see us when you're walking
again?'

'Yes, of course.' Yvette forgot her own troubles
in the face of this widow's brave acceptance of hers.
'Are you strong enough?'

Janine nodded. 'I would have been home by now
in the ordinary way but Sister Jeanne wouldn't let
me. They've been very good to me here but I must
learn to live alone.'

Yvette felt ashamed of her own paltry worries.
'Perhaps you'll marry again,' she suggested, and
thought of Daniel. 'There are a great many men
. . .'

'Yes, I know,' Janine interrupted, 'but I won't
rush into anything. I want a quiet man, a gentle
man, a friend, someone I can talk to.'

That struck a chord of memory in Yvette. That
was exactly what Daniel had said about the woman
he wanted. She hid a smile.

Janine was speaking again after burping her
baby. 'Georges was a good man, I suppose,' she
said softly so that the other young mothers in the
room could not hear. 'He provided well for me.'
She hesitated. 'I don't wish to speak ill of the dead,
especially since he did such a brave thing in fighting
the Indians, but he was a violent man.'

Yvette had a sudden picture of a frightened
Janine drawing back from that violence directed
towards her. Marriage was not always as girls im-
agined it would be. She shivered. How did one

know what qualities a man would display towards a wife—until too late?

'You were given the King's Dowry to come here, weren't you, Janine?' she asked.

'Yes, I was an orphan and I came for the dowry and a home of my own that would be warm and loving like the home I remembered from long ago. I tried to please Georges, but he was a drinking man and rough with it.' Janine smiled down at her baby. 'It'll be different now. I shall be good and gentle towards my little Francine.' Then she looked up at Yvette. 'I must speak to someone,' she went on. 'Don't think badly of me—and promise not to tell anyone—but I feel such a cheat. They all say I'm brave. I'm not. Is it wrong for me to be happy? I have my baby and my home.'

'No, of course not, but surely all men aren't like Georges?' Yvette wanted to be reassured.

Janine shot her a shrewd look. 'Some are kind. You don't know Madame Richard? Her husband was kind and they had four children. He drowned last year and within a week of his death she had three proposals. I asked her how she would decide. I thought she might take the richest—but she chose the poorest and the kindest. They seem very happy and such good friends,' she smiled shyly at Yvette. 'It's September now,' she continued softly, 'but in the winter cold it would be good to have a man to cut the wood and clear the snow and be company for me and baby.' She left the words hanging in the air.

With all her talk of not rushing into another

marriage, it was clear to Yvette that Janine would find another man, and she was almost sure who that man would be. After all, what else was there for a woman? It was nature's way. Her own mother had found that when she had taken a lover after so many years on her own.

That afternoon, Captain Renaud was the first veranda visitor. Madame Brun-Cartier, who had napped the best part of the morning away, was fast asleep again so they were able to speak.

'Your friend was very upset,' the Captain told Yvette. 'I don't think she'll ever do it again.' He was very serious. 'Though she had been foolish I felt sorry for her. She told me she had never had anything and I knew she spoke the truth. No girl would come here to claim the King's Dowry if any other course were open to her.'

'That's true,' Yvette agreed fervently.

'Was it so with you?' the Captain asked. 'Somehow you don't give the impression of such poverty as hers.'

Yvette sat back in surprise. 'I didn't know you ever thought about me to wonder how I felt.' She clasped her hands and added, almost to herself, 'or where I came from.'

Alain was perched on the veranda rail looking down at her. 'I'm human, am I not? Why shouldn't I wonder about you? In you I see a girl of some contradictions; clearly you're more than a farm girl or an orphanage girl. You have a mind of your own, a kind of confidence in yourself and a ready wit. You're brave and sensible and willing to work and to help others— and you're pretty as well.'

Yvette blushed with pleasure to hear he thought well of her.

His eyes looked steadily into hers. 'What drove you out from France? A man?'

Yvette's eyes dropped to her clasped hands. It would be easy to tell Alain in this soft mood the whole story. 'My mother died,' she began. 'She was a dressmaker and we made a good living.'

Madame Brun-Cartier stirred and yawned. 'What's that you say? A dressmaker? But we all know that.' Her dark eyes snapped. 'What was your mother, Captain? A lady?'

He nodded. 'The Lady Madeleine. She was a beautiful woman—blonde like Liliane and with eyes the same shade of blue.'

Yvette understood now, or thought she did. Liliane reminded him of his mother. That was why he had done so much for her.

Alain continued, 'She died when I was five, but I remember her kissing me goodnight and comforting me when I hurt myself.'

Unbidden, a picture of a lonely little Alain presented itself to Yvette: a little motherless boy missing the beautiful Lady Madeleine, and crying himself to sleep.

'Why did you join the army?' asked Madame, breaking into that moment. 'Other careers must have been open to you.'

Alain shrugged. 'I was a second son. In our family the second son went into the army. My father bought my commission. I fought in Europe and when the regiment was sent to New France I came too.'

He might have said more, indeed in this mood Yvette felt sure he would have explained more about himself, but they were interrupted.

Marc Barbier came round the corner of the veranda. 'What, only the good Captain Renaud here today?' He bowed to Madame and kissed Yvette's hand.

'I'm just going,' said Alain. 'I shall look in on my man.' He left them as Marc sat down in a comfortable chair.

'Have you heard the news, ladies?'

'What news?' they both asked.

'First the news about Guillaume,' he announced shaking his head at Yvette. 'I'm afraid he's not going to wait to see if the Captain bestows your hand upon him. He's busy harvesting now and his neighbour has promised to take care of his livestock for a few weeks. Guillaume has heard there's another bride ship coming in the next few weeks, and he's off for Québec and a bride as soon as he can.'

'Good luck to him,' exclaimed Yvette, but she couldn't help remembering Madame Brun-Cartier's words about things changing. They were changing indeed—first Daniel, now Guillaume—the men were melting away.

Marc laughed at the expression on her face. He patted her hand. 'Never mind, I'm still here, though I'm not so sure about your Captain.'

'What do you mean?' asked Yvette. 'He isn't my Captain.'

'I'm glad to hear you say that,' Marc smiled. 'I understand his eye is upon your little friend Liliane these days. He called on her the other night and helped her to move some of her things to the chocolate shop—she's working there.'

'Yes, I'd heard about the shop,' Yvette admitted. 'She came to tell me herself.'

'But not about the Captain, I'll be bound,' Marc was still smiling.

There was no answering smile from Yvette. She felt unaccountably saddened, thinking that Alain had said Liliane had reminded him of his mother.

'It's all over the town,' Marc continued. 'She's telling everyone Captain Renaud is taking care of her and that both of them are going to the Governor's Ball. How would you ladies like to go too?'

'Don't be silly,' declared Madame Brun-Cartier, suddenly taking part in the conversation. 'We're hospital patients—how can we go to any ball?'

'Quite easily,' Marc responded. 'Look.' He drew two small envelopes from his pocket and handed one to each of them.

Yvette fingered hers and then ripped it open. It was an invitation to the Governor's Ball on Friday.

'I shall escort you both.' He held up his hand to still Madame's protests.

Yvette made no protest at all. She didn't care if she was still on crutches. She had an invitation and she was determined to attend. She didn't even care that it was delivered much later than Liliane's or Pauline's. But what would she wear?

She and Madame were discussing that very point heatedly when Alain reappeared and asked what was happening.

He frowned when they told him, all speaking at once. 'Is it wise?' he asked, and both ladies turned on him.

'Wise?' asked Madame Brun-Cartier. 'This young man is to escort us. I'm old and infirm but I'm not ill—I'll thank you to remember that.'

'Wise?' echoed Yvette. 'I have a broken leg—it's not contagious—you needn't fear you'll catch it.'

It was useless for the Captain to reply to that. He looked from Madame to the girl. 'My apologies,' he said stiffly. 'I did not mean to imply anything of the kind.'

'*You're* going, aren't you?' asked Yvette. 'But you did not think of taking us.' She might have added 'with Liliane', but a quick look at Alain's face stopped the words before her tongue uttered them. She looked at Marc and rose to her feet.

'Thank you, Marc, we shall be delighted to attend the ball.' She threw her arms around him and hugged him. 'Thank you, thank you.' Never mind what Alain thought of that. He probably got all the hugs he wanted from Liliane.

CHAPTER
NINE

ON MONDAY afternoon the carriage came as promised for Yvette. She had Madame Archambault's finished dress neatly parcelled and was eager to deliver it.

When she arrived at the governor's house, Marc was waiting for her and showed her into the same downstairs parlour as he had that first day. He handed her into a brocade chair.

'I wanted to talk to you,' he declared. 'Promise you won't be angry with me.'

'Why should I be angry?' She was puzzled.

'Just promise.'

'All right, I promise,' Yvette agreed, intrigued by this air of secrecy.

'I went to see the furrier,' Marc began. 'Your jacket is coming along well. I told him to go ahead and fit the lining—that I'd be responsible for paying him.'

'But you can't do that,' Yvette protested.

'Why not?' Marc bestowed a winning smile on her. 'I wanted to please you. I asked him to have it ready for later this week. I know Madame Brun-Cartier is lending you a dress for the ball. Every girl likes to make an impression when she arrives at a party. Admit you'll love sweeping in to the ball-room wearing a beautiful dress and a beaver jacket. What an accomplishment for a girl on her own, in a new country only a few weeks, and by her own efforts.' He dropped into a chair facing her and took her hand in his.

'Of course I'd love it,' Yvette had no difficulty convincing herself of that and she felt warmed by his praise. 'And I'll need some kind of wrap as the evenings are chilly. But a girl shouldn't accept a gift like that from a man—it's too personal.'

Marc laughed softly, 'It's only the lining we're talking about, after all. What a little innocent you are. I'm just helping you to look your best so I can be proud of you.' He stroked her hand. 'Girls accept all sorts of personal gifts from men. They don't have to talk about them. It'll just be be-tween you and me. We're old friends, aren't we? Our families knew each other in Sainte-Agathe.'

Yvette was sorely tempted. 'That was just a story we made up on the ship.'

'A good story,' Marc still held her hand. 'I've grown to believe it. I feel we were childhood friends and, for the sake of that friendship, accept my gift, please, just as you accepted my invitation and my escort to the ball.'

Yvette glanced at his laughing blue eyes and looked away. 'If it's offered only in friendship,' she said with some hesitation.

'What else, Yvette?' he asked quietly. 'Have I demanded anything else?'

'No,' she admitted and met his eyes. 'But generally when men give presents they expect something in return.'

'Oh-ho,' exclaimed Marc, dropping her hand, 'what do you think I want?'

'I'm not sure,' she replied, half feeling this man was dangerous.

'Have I ever acted improperly towards you?' He rose to his feet and stood above her.

'No,' Yvette was quite sure of that. 'You've been a good friend to me and I've enjoyed your company.'

'Well, then, why do you doubt me now?' he demanded, gesturing largely with his arms. 'I'm as I've always been. I'm asking nothing in return.' He took a step away and then whirled back. 'Is that it? You want me to ask for something?'

'No, yes, I don't know,' Yvette replied. After all, Marc had been visiting her at the hospital for some weeks. She had thought of him as one of her suitors. Was he telling her he wasn't? Alain had said Marc would never marry her. How could she explain that to him? 'It's . . . just . . .' she paused.

'You can't believe in my good nature,' Marc suggested.

'Something like that,' she agreed.

'That's not very flattering.' He perched on a large pouffe in front of her. 'I thought we were friends.'

'We are friends.' Yvette was still puzzled and troubled.

'So, it's settled,' he patted her knee. 'You'll accept,' he smiled, 'and by the way you can drop in for a fitting with the fur man after Madame has finished with you.'

'All right,' Yvette made up her mind suddenly. 'I'll accept, and thank you very much, Marc.'

'My pleasure,' he told her and rose to his feet. 'It'll be our secret.' He held out his hand to her to help her up. 'I'll introduce you to my friends at the ball. You'll have a splendid time and you must save the first dance for me—and the last.'

'You're going too fast,' said Yvette. 'Even if the splints are off, I may not be able to dance right away.'

'Nonsense.' Marc put his finger against her mouth in an endearing way and rubbed it gently. 'You'll dance with me.'

Yvette began to believe it herself, Marc was so positive. She followed him up the stairs to Madame Archambault's quarters and he left her at the door.

Madame tried on the dress immediately and was delighted with it. 'It's just as I hoped it would be,' she told the girl. 'You are a clever little cousin. If you want to set up as a dressmaker here you'll have no trouble at all. Just to show you how pleased I am I mean to give you a little more than the agreed price. You'll be able to afford the lining for your jacket now.' Madame took up her purse and paid Yvette then and there. 'I hear you're coming to the ball. I've told my husband all about you and he's looking forward to meeting you. Remember you are my second cousin Anne-Marie's daughter—and she is my second cousin once removed.'

With great good-will on both sides they parted company, and Yvette thought it strange that both Marc and Madame wanted to pay for her lining. She went to call on the furrier, still pensive.

He was all attention and she tried on the nearly completed garment and was thrilled with it. The hat was also most becoming, and Yvette found herself in a most agreeable humour about the whole project.

Since the carriage appeared to be hers to command, she popped into Leger's chocolate shop, where Liliane greeted her with enthusiasm.

She had heard Yvette was going to the ball and wanted to know what she was going to wear.

Yvette was able to tell her that Madame Brun-Cartier, after first saying she couldn't go, wouldn't go, had suddenly decided she could and would and had offered Yvette a bronze-coloured satin dress which she was in the process of remodelling now. She was on her way to Michelin's to buy some lace for the bodice, she was delighted to add.

'Madame Brun-Cartier is wearing wine-coloured velvet,' she went on. 'Do you know she brought a trunk full of clothes to the hospital? She hasn't worn one of them since she's been there. I had a splendid time choosing a beautiful frock.'

With some of the extra money Madame Archambault had given her Yvette bought chocolates as a gift for Madame Brun-Cartier. It was wonderful to have money she had earned. Then she proceded to Michelin's.

Pauline was nowhere in evidence and Monsieur Michelin himself served her. He soon found exactly the right shade of apricot lace and also suggested some ribbon for trimming. The price was within her means.

Well satisfied, she returned to the hospital and to Madame Brun-Cartier's thanks for the sweets. She started work on her ball-gown singing. She was changing the neckline completely and altering the fit of the skirt. There was a considerable amount of work involved but she was confident it would be a very presentable dress.

'Janine is going home by the end of the week,' Madame reported, 'and one of the others by the beginning of next. It's all changing, just as I was getting used to them. It will be the same with you,' she sighed. 'You'll marry and I'll never see you again.'

'Oh Madame,' Yvette assured her, 'I shall come to visit you and bring you chocolates—if I've enough money.'

'*Peut-être*; that's what you say now', was the gloomy reply, and the old woman refused to be cheered.

Yvette was so busy with her dress that she almost forgot about her leg. Certainly she forgot to worry about it.

On the Wednesday afternoon Sister Jeanne called her into the small office and announced, 'We'll take off the splints,' and proceeded to do so.

Yvette couldn't believe it. She held her breath and shut her eyes and prayed, a swift wish that all would be well.

'Ah,' exclaimed Sister Jeanne as she loosened the bindings and the splints fell away.

Still Yvette's eyes remained shut. She felt the nun's hands on her leg.

'Open your eyes and look,' Sister Jeanne instructed her.

Yvette did so. Was that her leg? That poor thing, thin and shrivelled and striped white and dirty in alternate rows where bear grease had reached.

'Is it all right?' she asked Sister Jeanne in a trembling whisper.

'The bone feels fine,' replied the nun, laughing at her expression. 'Put your foot on the floor and try it.'

Gingerly, Yvette extended her foot and stood up, holding her skirts high. 'It feels shorter than the other one,' she exclaimed.

'Of course it will,' Sister Jeanne said. 'You have a shoe on the other foot. Try walking.'

Yvette took a step, one hand leaning on the back of the chair.

The nun watched her encouragingly. 'I thought you couldn't wait to walk on your own,' she teased.

Yvette let go of the chair back and took another step and another. 'I can walk,' she cried. 'I can really walk, but it hurts.' She came back abruptly to the chair and sat down.

'It's bound to ache.' The nun seemed to find this amusing. 'You haven't used it for a long time.' She felt the bone again. 'There's nothing to worry about. It has healed well. It will take time to regain your confidence and for the muscles to become supple again. You'll want to take it easy for a day or two but you're cured physically. It takes a while for the mind to accept that. Now believe it and thank God. Off you go and show your friends.'

That was what Yvette did. She thanked God and she thanked Sister Jeanne. Then she walked across the hall to the women's ward. Janine and the other girls and Sister Marie made a great fuss over her.

Madame Brun-Cartier smiled, then added, 'I suppose you won't sit with me any more on the veranda now.'

Yvette hugged her and promised that of course she would. That was where both of them were going now, and when the Captain came later on Madame was to say nothing and suddenly Yvette would get up and walk and surprise him; that is if the Captain came, and after yesterday she wasn't at all sure of that.

Madame agreed to that plan and the two of them waited all the rest of the afternoon on the veranda, Yvette still busy with the ball-gown.

Daniel showed up around four and she surprised him. He made her walk up and down but he didn't stay long. He went in to see Francine and her mother on his way out.

Yvette was still sure the Captain would come, but where was he? Was he with Liliane? She wondered that to herself, but Madame wondered it out loud.

'Just like a man,' she declared. 'When you want him, he isn't there.'

At last Yvette was forced to admit he wasn't coming that afternoon and, as it was becoming chilly outside, they moved indoors. He would have come if he could, she told herself, but she was disappointed and deflated. Perhaps he was cross about her going to the ball with Marc, and was punishing her. She sighed. Perhaps he'd come tomorrow. Why was she so disappointed anyway? She only wanted to show him she was independent now. But there was no Captain Renaud again tomorrow. Neither did any of the other men call.

Yvette finished her dress and told herself she had needed that uninterrupted time, but she was vaguely unhappy though her leg looked much healthier now. She had washed away the dirt and the grease; Sister Marie had given her some lotion and helped her to massage it, and she had begun to conquer the feeling that her leg would somehow give way under her if she used it too much.

Then it was Friday, the day of the ball.

There was a tin bath in the hospital which Yvette had often looked at longingly. Now she brought it to her little cell of a room and she and Sister Marie poured hot water into it and the good nun produced some fine soap, a present from a grateful patient.

Yvette hadn't had a proper bath since before she left France. She revelled in the hot water and the freedom of her leg. It was even beginning to look like her own leg and to feel as though it belonged to her. She sang as she soaped herself. She washed her hair too.

Afterwards, dressed in her oldest cotton frock, she sat outside on a tree-stump in the garden drying her hair.

It was there Marc found her. She heard the carriage and saw him and jumped up to meet him.

'You're walking,' he exclaimed, and left the moving carriage in one quick leap to hug her. Then they danced about in a circle holding hands while the coachman watched smiling.

Someone else watched too—a horseman. Yvette suddenly became conscious of that. She looked up laughing, her untied hair free and wild about her face in the breeze.

It was Captain Renaud mounted on a large black horse, a frowning Captain Renaud.

Yvette dropped Marc's hand and tried to straighten her hair.

'She's walking,' announced Marc.

'So I see,' replied the Captain. 'Congratulations, Mademoiselle. I'm pleased it has turned out well for you. I had meant to be here when it happened. I shall see you tonight and talk to you.' He saluted her and wheeled his horse about.

'Whew, frosty, wasn't he?' exclaimed Marc. 'Is he always so stiff and correct with you?'

'No, not always', replied Yvette, remembering times when Alain had held her in his arms—when he had kissed her. 'Why couldn't he have come yesterday?' Did he kiss Liliane too?

Marc laughed at her. 'He was out on some sort of patrol or hunt—I'm not sure which. He's a very active man, our Captain. Perhaps he didn't like to see you in your house-frock with your hair unpinned, dancing on the grass with me.' He captured her hand again. 'I've never seen you look prettier.' He led her to the carriage. 'I've brought your beaver jacket.' He reached under the seat and handed it to her. 'Take it in and try it on. I shall wait till tonight to see you in all your finery.' He jumped into the carriage and waved goodbye, and Yvette shook out the jacket and pressed the fur against her face.

The afternoon seemed to go on forever. Madame Brun-Cartier dozed on the veranda and Yvette tried to follow her example, but she was too excited by the thought of the ball.

She supposed she should be thinking about the future now that her leg was better, but the only future she wanted to think about was the ball tonight and her bronze dress and beaver jacket and how she'd look wearing them.

It was warm on the veranda until just before four, but then the sun suddenly went behind a cloud and Yvette woke Madame and shepherded her inside, determined she should not take a chill before evening.

As they went in, Daniel drew up with a horse and cart.

'I've come to take Janine to her home,' he said. 'Her neighbour is there now and has everything ready.'

Yvette realised she hadn't even said goodbye to baby Francine. She went in to help and Madame to supervise. Everyone was saying goodbye and good luck to Janine, and Yvette kissed her and was allowed to carry Francine to the cart and hand her to her mother.

'I shall be fine,' Janine told Sister Jeanne, who had also come out. 'I have good neighbours.'

Daniel tied the goat securely in the back of the cart and with Janine and the baby beside him on the driver's bench and the nanny bleating away in the back they drove off waving to everyone.

'It's all changing, just like Madame Brun-Cartier said,' Yvette reflected to herself. 'I shall be leaving too, one day soon . . . but I won't think of that now. It was kind of Daniel to come for Janine. I suppose it's because he has a horse and cart and not everyone has.'

When Marc called that evening, Yvette and Madame Brun-Cartier were ready. Madame, in putting on her wine velvet, had shed ten years. Amélie, one of the little mothers, had helped her to dress and done her hair, and then had combed and brushed Yvette's brown curls so they fell in soft corkscrews round her face, secured by the angel combs, and were gathered in large loose ringlets tied with a bronze bow at the back of her head.

'Such beautiful hair,' said Amélie, 'so thick and willing. Now, then, stand up and let me see the whole effect.' She set the two candles on the table further apart so that the light fell properly on Yvette and surveyed her. 'Beautiful,' was her hushed verdict.

Yvette looked at herself and drew in her breath. She had never had anything that suited her so well as the bronze satin, exactly the colour of her eyes, and her hair was so flatteringly arranged. She couldn't believe it was herself. Wide-eyed the girl in the mirror stared back at her, lips parted in anticipation.

'Now the jacket,' instructed Amélie, her hand lingering on the soft fur.

Yvette put it on and sighed with pleasure. It was perfect. 'I'm afraid,' she told Amélie.

'Afraid of what?' The other looked at her in astonishment.

'I've never looked like this before or been dressed like this. Perhaps it will all disappear.'

Amélie sat down and laughed. 'It won't disappear. Go and have a good time, you silly goose. I wish I were going to a ball.' She shooed her out of the room.

*   *   *

It was in some ways a magical evening. Marc told her how magnificent she looked, that any man would be proud to escort her. Her fur jacket was exactly right for the open carriage this evening. Madame Brun-Cartier was wrapped up in blankets against the night air but Yvette, sitting beside Marc, with the stars glowing brightly in a velvet sky and a thin sliver of moon casting a pale radiance over the quiet town, was warm and cosy in her beaver. It was a time for dreams.

They were received by a liveried footman at the governor's door, and Yvette was so in love with her new jacket that she didn't want to part with it. However, she allowed a servant to take it and place it in the cloakroom.

They proceeded towards the receiving line in the ballroom—a room of exquisite taste in pale blue and gold which Yvette had never seen before. She admired the chandeliers with hundreds of candles and the mirrors in the alcoves. The orchestra was playing softly and Marc was teasing Madame about being the belle of the evening.

Yvette saw Alain, and suddenly the beauty of the room was forgotten as he smiled and came towards her. Her pulse quickened, she felt her lips respond in a welcoming smile. Her whole being lit up and she knew in that instant a devastating truth. She loved Alain. There was no hint of uncertainty or doubt about that. She caught her breath. It was impossible. He didn't love her, didn't want to marry her. She faced the fact squarely—she loved

Alain. She didn't know when it had happened, why it had happened, but there was no way she could deny it or even, tonight at least, regret it.

She took a step towards him gladly and her hands were clasped in his.

'*Belle, enchantantée!*' he exclaimed. 'You're truly beautiful with your amber dress and amber eyes,' and he hummed a few bars of the song he had sung about the amber-eyed girl on the night of the picnic on *Le Poisson Bleu*.

He stayed beside her and put his name on her dance programme for three dances, even though Marc frowned at him.

By this time Madame Brun-Cartier was being introduced to the dignitaries in the receiving line, and Yvette found her hand taken by Monsieur Archambault who bestowed a very friendly smile on her and said he was enchanted to meet his wife's little cousin at last and he hoped that she would keep a rein on Marc.

Yvette wasn't quite sure what to make of this remark but she smiled and said she'd try, since that seemed to be what he wanted to hear. Then her hand was taken by the governor's wife.

'I've heard all about you and your cleverness with the needle. Madame Archambault's dress is splendid. Doesn't it suit her, and so nice to see her out of mourning, such an attractive woman.'

It was true. She looked at Madame Archambault just a little further down the line and flushed with pleasure at the praise.

'You're the little bride with the broken leg,' the governor broke in. 'All better now? And is this young man to be congratulated?' He indicated Marc.

Before Yvette could deal with that, Madame Archambault took hold of her and kissed her cheek. They looked at each other with appreciation.

'Flair, definitely you have flair,' Madame decided. 'I thought so when I first saw you. Turn round and let me see the back of your dress.'

Yvette twirled round. Madame Archambault nodded in approval: 'Quite charming.'

'You look lovely, Madame,' Yvette said. Then Marc claimed her for the first dance while Alain led Madame Brun-Cartier out.

'They're all busy linking our names together,' Marc whispered in her ear.

'Do you think so?' Yvette nearly missed her step. If there was one thing she didn't want now it was any kind of declaration from Marc until she had sorted out her feelings. 'Look, there's Liliane over there, and Pauline, don't they look grand? Liliane's with Nicholas, the brewer.'

'The perfect couple,' observed Marc. 'She'll talk and he'll listen.'

The steps of the dance carried her apart from Marc and by the time they came together again the music had ended and Alain claimed Yvette for the next one. This was slower and she could allow herself the luxury and excitement of feeling Alain's arm around her waist, his body near hers. Her steps matched his and melted into them. What pleasure it was to be here with him. She sighed, and he smiled down at her.

'It's good to see you dancing,' he exclaimed, 'but do you know I almost miss the scent of bear grease.'

'I don't,' laughed Yvette. 'But it did work. I gave my crutches to Sister Jeanne for the next broken leg.'

'Let's forget all that.' Alain stood back and bowed to her in the intricate pattern of the dance. 'It's a night for enjoyment, for laughter.' He pulled her close again. 'I saw you in your fur jacket when you came in. It suits you very well. None of your companions from the ship have coats like that, such as a princess might envy—or smiling eyes like yours,' he added softly. 'Pretty little Yvette, are you still angry with me for keeping you from the Choosing?'

Yvette shook her head and her eyes held his. For a moment she allowed herself the bliss of feeling he liked her. If only he loved her as she loved him. She wanted time to stay still so that she might be held there in his arms, but the music stopped too soon and another officer claimed her for a partner. She was whirled from one set of arms to another. Admiring men were everywhere, eager to dance and flirt with her. As the only unattached single girl there, she was complimented and teased and sought after.

It was truly the ball of every girl's dreams for her—or would have been if only Alain loved her. She saw him dancing with Pauline and then Liliane, and even Madame Archambault and the governor's wife, and she envied each of them.

At supper-time, she ate with Marc, Madame Brun-Cartier and Alain at the governor's table. Liliane was with Nicholas. It was a delicious repast of cold meats and vol-au-vents with mushrooms and eels, and there was smoked meat and fish and sweet cakes and pastries accompanied with wine. They all made her feel very welcome and accepted. Monsieur Archambault asked about the second cousin Anne-Patrice and Yvette corrected him gently and said it was Anne-Marie, and she was a cousin twice removed.

After the meal, when the dancing resumed, Alain claimed his second dance. If it had been anyone else she would have put him off, because while sitting down to eat, her leg had begun to bother her. Perhaps if she leaned against him a little, the pain would go away.

'Are you tired?' he asked her. 'Is your leg aching?'

'A little,' she admitted. 'It's not used to dancing.' She tried to make light of it. 'I long to put it up and rub it for a while, but that's impossible,' she laughed ruefully.

'Why is it?' he asked. 'Come with me,' he suggested, 'and we'll find a place where I shall sit down and talk to you.' He led her from the ballroom and down the corridor and, taking a candle from its holder on the wall, opened a door.

Yvette recognised it as the room Marc had brought her to on her first visit there. She sank onto a small settee and raised her leg thankfully along it.

Alain put the candlestick down on a small ornate table and gathered several cushions. These he placed under her leg, and he perched on the edge of the settee to massage it.

'Wonderful!' Yvette relaxed under his touch, his fingers easing cramped muscles. 'That's just what it needed.' She was content now. 'How do you know just what to do?' she asked.

'Soldiers soon learn about sore muscles and wounds and broken bones,' he told her.

'Were you wounded often?' asked Yvette.

'I've been lucky,' Alain went on kneading her leg. 'I had a gash deep in my leg and a sword-stroke that broke my shoulder bone. The surgeon advised massage for that.'

His head was bent to his soothing and Yvette longed to put out her hand and touch his hair. Would it be soft—that thick fair mane of his that glowed in the candlelight? Almost of its own volition her hand went out, but a noise in the corridor caused her to withdraw it.

She heard the words, 'We'll be private in here,' in a woman's voice, and the door opened.

Marc and Madame Archambault stood there. His arm was round her waist, her face upturned to his.

For a moment they stood motionless. Then Marc spoke. 'Someone's here before us. Our good Captain Renaud is playing doctor and patient.' He pulled Madame Archambault forward and they entered the room, closing the door behind them.

Marc and Madame sat down side by side on small gold chairs facing Yvette.

Yvette turned hot and cold. 'My leg was aching,' she stammered. Alain's hand still rested on it.

Marc began to laugh. It was not his usual chuckling laugh but a laugh with a sneer to it.

What would have happened then, what would have been said, Yvette had no idea, for the door was flung open and Monsieur Archambault stood there.

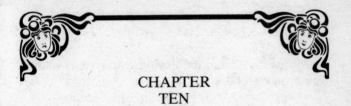

CHAPTER
TEN

MONSIEUR Archambault had come into the salon and simply taken charge. He had summoned servants to bring hot towels and cold towels for Yvette's leg and then had insisted that a bed be made up for her upstairs and that she should spend the night there.

Marc was despatched to escort Madame Brun-Cartier back to the hospital. Captain Renaud went with them, probably to set Sister Jeanne's mind at rest.

Yvette's protests about being the cause of so much upset and inconvenience were totally ignored. Monsieur Archambault was a man so used to commanding that he was not to be diverted.

The girl found herself upstairs, undressed, tucked into a flannel nightgown and in bed in a very short space of time. There was a warming-pan and the mattress was soft and comfortable. The bed had been made with clean scented sheets and an eider-down.

A servant brought her hot chocolate mixed with some kind of wine, and despite the strangeness of her surroundings she fell asleep almost at once.

There was no hospital stir to awaken her and she slept on till a roll and tea were brought to her on a tray.

'Monsieur Archambault says you are to rest until lunch-time and then he wishes to speak to you,' the servant informed her before she slipped away.

Yvette ate her breakfast in comfort and then found herself wide awake and curious about her leg. It ached a little and she experimented with standing on it and walking about the room. It was a little stiff, but that was all. A great deal of fuss had surely been made about nothing.

It was a pretty room with a warm red carpet with white and black flowers, a white wall, and chintz curtains at the windows which looked out on the back gardens. There were turnips and cabbages and apple trees in the distance.

Yvette sat for a long time in the chair by the window, wrapped in the eiderdown from the bed just looking and allowing the morning peace and green of that outside world where birds sang and the river gleamed silver in the distance to enter into her. Strangely, she had no fear of whatever Monsieur Archambault might have to say to her. Nor did she brood on what had happened last night. Her mind had blocked it all out. She must have been more tired than she knew, for she dozed again and woke only when the servant brought water for washing and a fresh brown and white checked gingham dress with a big white collar.

The woman helped her to dress and even provided soft shoes before leading her to the dining-room. Yvette dined alone on soup and cold meats and fresh bread.

Madame Archambault, it seemed, was spending the day in bed and Monsieur was lunching with the governor.

When Yvette was finishing this pleasant but solitary repast Marc came in and sat down opposite her, helping himself to bread and meat.

'You don't seem out of place here,' he commented, signalling to the footman to fill his glass with wine. 'But then I should have known you wouldn't be.'

Yvette was surprised. 'Because I am a dress-maker's daughter, you mean? I never knew you felt that way.'

'What way?' Marc parried quickly.

'That we're of a different class—superiors and inferiors, rich and poor, I suppose.' Yvette sighed. 'I just liked you for yourself, because you made me laugh, because you liked me.' Even as she spoke she knew her relationship, whatever it had been, with Marc was over after last night.

'I still like you,' Marc protested.

'Yes,' Yvette agreed, her mind clear on that. 'But not enough.'

'Perhaps more than you think,' he told her. 'I enjoyed your company and I thought I might turn that to my advantage.' He sipped the wine. 'A married man would have been more acceptable to Monsieur Archambault.' He raised his hand at her expression. 'No, no, nothing has been said and it's better that way. I have asked for a transfer to Québec and Monsieur is quite willing to do anything in his power to assist me in that.' He speared a piece of cheese.

'I'll miss you. When will you go?' Yvette took a bite of apple.

'Next week, the week after. I don't suppose you'd fancy Québec?'

She shook her head.

'After the Captain, are you?' He helped himself to more bread. 'Sure he'll suit you? His family are even grander than mine.' His eyes were bright with amusement. 'After last night, he'll feel he has to offer for you. Clever little Yvette, you managed better than I did.' He held up his hand. 'I shouldn't tell him about the lining, though.'

'What do you mean?' Yvette choked on her apple, her mouth suddenly dry. 'How have I been clever?'

'You're smart enough to know that Monsieur Archambault has taken you under his wing and means to see you respectably married. I think he feels that any man who puts a finger on his wife's second cousin—even though twice removed—is answerable to him, and our good Captain was rubbing your leg with some enthusiasm.'

'But you were there,' Yvette protested, 'and Madame.'

Marc smiled at her. 'A little late in the day, my dear—and he knows that too. Oh, he's grateful to you.' He examined an apple, then discarded it in favour of a plum. 'The presence of you and Alain prevented a nasty scandal. I'm grateful, too,' Marc winked at her. 'He'll see the Captain does the right thing by you. Lucky Yvette, your heart's desire delivered on a plate.' With a flourish he offered her a plum.

Yvette refused it. She couldn't have tasted it, let alone swallowed it. 'I don't want him that way,' she murmured through stiff lips.

Marc looked at her, another fruit half-way to his lips. 'That's stupid pride talking. Think about your choices if you don't take him. You'll be married out of hand to someone like the silent Nicholas or that poor lost lad Guillaume.' There was a hint of pity in his tone underneath the banter. 'Alain may fight against it at first, but you're a pretty girl, a girl with a lovely body, you'll win him round.'

If anything, the thought of using her body to win Alain round was even more distasteful to Yvette than the idea of Monsieur Archambault forcing the marriage on him. But Yvette recognised all too well that she could be pushed into a marriage she did not want at all.

Marc had helped himself to an apple. The thought of parting from Madame Archambault had evidently not affected his appetite, but Yvette left her apple uneaten on the plate while she tried to reach some sort of decision.

'Oh, by the way,' said Marc, 'Monsieur Archambault won't be through till nearly three. He'll see you in the little parlour then. If you want to take a walk in the garden or sit in the sun, you're at liberty to do so. Do you want that apple?' He indicated the one lying on the plate with just one bite taken from it.

When she shook her head he put the fruit on his plate and cut round the bite. 'Dancing always makes me hungry.' He finished it, then stood up and put his hand on her shoulder. 'Cheer up, you'll be grateful to Monsieur Archambault yet. I shouldn't wonder if he were to give you a wedding present as well. After all, a second cousin is still a blood relation.'

Yvette managed a wan smile and a wave as Marc left. She only wished she could accept her situation as easily as Marc had done. She sat at the table staring into space, her mind going round in circles. The servants seemed to have forgotten her. No one came to clear the table. It was very quiet, so quiet that she might have been alone in this big establishment, as alone as she would be married to Captain Renaud in an alliance that he resented.

No, it was unthinkable. She would not have him that way. He must come freely to her or not at all. She shuddered at the misery of that thought.

One thing was certain. She would not sit meekly here waiting for a man she barely knew to decide her fate. She would put aside all thought of marriage and make her own way in Ville-Marie. Her mother had made a living as a dressmaker—well, so would she. The King could keep his dowry. If she went back to the hospital she knew Sister Jeanne would try to talk her out of that resolve. There was one course open to her. Janine lived alone with her baby and had said she did not mean to rush into marriage again. She would go to her and ask if she could share her home. She would help with the chores, and gradually as the money came in from her expanding business she would pay board. Yvette didn't doubt for a moment that she would succeed. Madame Archambault's dress had been greatly admired last night.

Now was the time for action. She would slip away before she was even missed—just find her jacket and go. She wouldn't risk going back upstairs. Her ball-gown was fair exchange for the dress she wore, but she would certainly not leave her beaver. She rose to her feet and went towards the cloakroom where she'd seen the servant take it the night before. It was still there.

With a thankful sigh, she patted it, then put it on. She went out of the big front door and no one was there to stop her. Let them all wonder where she was and make their plans without her. She had plans for herself and needed time to get them under way.

Fortunately she had a fairly clear idea of the location of Janine's house and decided the sensible thing to do was not to go through the main street of the town but to walk purposefully along the upper street that ran parallel to it. She knew that only houses lay along that way, and who would notice her? If she was seen, anyone would think she was a girl calling on a friend or neighbour.

This strategy worked well. No one challenged her. Indeed no one was in the street and she followed it to the corner where it joined the main street on the edge of town. She could see the saw-mill from there, and a small boy sitting on a fence told her which house was Janine's. By now, she was carrying her jacket because it was so warm.

She went up the path to the door and Janine was standing there and welcomed her.

'I didn't expect to see you so soon,' she exclaimed, hugging her. 'Are you alone? Come in and sit down and tell me all about the dance.'

Yvette poured it all out and finished by asking if she could remain. 'We shall be two against the world,' she pointed out.

'And company for each other,' agreed Janine. 'I welcome the idea, but are you sure you want to set yourself against authority? It won't be easy to be on your own.'

Yvette was sure and soon convinced Janine.

'You must tell someone you are here,' Janine declared.

'Not yet.' Yvette shook her head, and the other could not persuade her on that score. 'I'll send a note to Sister Jeanne tomorrow or the next day when they've cooled down, and in the meantime I'll draw up a notice of my charges to interest some of the ladies in the town about having clothes made for them. After all, at the hospital they think I'm at the governor's. At the governor's, they'll suppose I'm back at Hôtel-Dieu.'

Since Yvette was so adamant, Janine gave way. Better to let her guest cool down as well. They spent a pleasant evening planning.

In the morning, as it was Sunday, Yvette volunteered to stay with Francine while Janine went to early Mass with one of the neighbours. She fed the baby and played with her. She was holding her in her arms when there was a knock on the door and Alain entered.

He filled the doorway, at once menacing and wrathful.

'I've been searching everywhere for you,' he exclaimed. 'Why did you run away without leaving a message?'

'I had to go.' Yvette clasped the baby to her.

'We've been up all night searching for you—afraid the Indians might have killed you or captured you. It's only because I went to very early Mass that I met Janine and she said you were here.' He sat down in the big rocking-chair.

'I'm sorry,' said Yvette, contrite now. 'I never thought anyone would bother.'

'How could we not bother—as you put it—after the attack on your little friend?' The Captain rubbed his hand across his eyes and Yvette couldn't help but notice how tired he looked. Her conscience smote her.

'I don't know why we bothered. The Indians are welcome to a thoughtless, selfish girl,' he went on angrily. 'Why should a patrol of soldiers be kept up all night?'

'I'm not selfish,' protested Yvette, stung by that thought, since she had left in order to spare him. She held Francine so tightly that the baby began to wail and she had to comfort her. 'I just wanted to get away.'

'Why was that?' asked Alain. 'Was the governor's house not comfortable? The bed not to your liking?'

Yvette shook her head.

'Well, what then?' Alain sat back and began to rock. 'Speak up or is it just that you don't want to tell me?'

Yvette was now so angry that she was trembling. 'I ran away so that I wouldn't have to marry you,' she snapped.

Alain jerked upright in his seat. 'That sounds extreme. I don't recall asking you to marry me. Did it slip my notice somehow?'

'No, you didn't ask me,' Yvette was close to tears. 'But I want you to know I wouldn't have you even if you did.'

'That's definite enough.' The Captain seemed singularly unperturbed by this piece of information.

'What's more,' Yvette rushed on, 'I don't intend to marry at all. I shall open a dressmaking business and manage on that, like my mother did before me.'

'You can't,' Alain was exasperatingly matter of

fact. 'There's the little matter of the King's Dowry.'

'The king can keep his dowry!' Yvette renounced her right to it in ringing tones.

'I'm afraid it's not as simple as that. You're just being a foolish girl.' Alain yawned hugely. 'You signed the papers agreeing to come.'

'I agreed to take part in the Choosing, like the other girls,' Yvette pointed out. 'You stopped me from doing that. You can make your explanations to the king about that.' Yvette felt a heady moment of triumph. She patted Francine on the back and the baby burped.

Alain looked at her. 'Well done, little one.' And Yvette almost smiled at him. He held up his hand. 'Can we stop arguing? You're safe. I'm hungry and tired and thirsty.'

'Would you like something to eat?' asked Yvette uncertainly.

'Yes, please.' He closed his eyes and sat back.

Yvette put Francine into her cradle and brought it near him. 'Just give it a little push if she cries,' she advised. 'I'll get you breakfast.'

Quickly she prepared bread, hot milk and an omelette.

Alain ate it all as though he were starving. 'I haven't had anything since lunch yesterday.' When he'd finished, he held out his cup for more and Yvette rose to refill it. She cut a slice of fruit cake as well. The neighbours had done their best for Janine and stocked her pantry.

By the time she returned to where Alain was

sitting before the fire, his eyes were closed, his feet stretched out. Both he and the baby in the cradle were fast asleep.

Yvette sank into a chair and watched him. Sprawled there, there was a defencelessness about him which was endearing. The lines of his face were smoothed away into boyishness. If only things had been different between them. She sighed and almost absently began to eat the cake and sip the cooling milk.

She didn't know how long she had been sitting there, but Janine's return from church roused her from her reverie.

'Let him sleep,' she exclaimed. 'The people next door are going to Mass now; go with them.'

Yvette slipped out and went to church. Perhaps some peace would be restored to her there. She would pray for strength not to be deflected from her purpose. She was sure it would not be right to trap Alain into marriage but it would be pleasanter if he wasn't so angry that he made her furious. She had been in the wrong, it seemed, to tell no one when she ran away. She saw that now. They must all have been worried to send out a search party. She must apologise for that. Gradually, as she followed the priest's action at the altar and listened to the sonorous Latin phrases, her feelings were soothed. She prayed for guidance and for help.

If the neighbours found her silent on the way back, they made no complaint but left her at the gate.

She had expected Alain to be gone, but he was still there, still asleep in the chair.

'He's doing no harm,' said Janine. 'Just sleeping as easily as the baby. We'll wake him for lunch presently.'

So the two girls prepared a meal. There was meat to roast and plenty of vegetables and they carried on a low-voiced conversation as they worked.

'It's good to have a man waiting for a meal.' Janine chopped onions with energy. 'I like to make a proper dinner. Yesterday I ate only scraps, just couldn't be bothered on my own.'

'You must take care of yourself.' Yvette was larding the meat. 'I shall have to see you do. Will he wake up as cross as he went to sleep?'

Janine laughed. 'We won't let him. I have some rhubarb wine. We'll open that to tempt him and there's apple tart to follow. You like him, don't you?'

'No, I don't.' Yvette put the meat in the oven, closing the door with a bang.

Janine only smiled. 'He must like you, too. He's followed you here. I always thought you'd make a match with him. He came to the hospital to see you often enough.'

'That didn't mean anything,' Yvette paused in her dicing of a turnip and held up the knife in the air. 'He just felt responsible for me.'

'He made himself responsible for you,' Janine corrected gently. 'And from what you told me last night he made himself responsible for Liliane for you. When all is ready here, you shall go in and wake him and smile at him and offer him a glass of wine. No one ever won a man by shouting at him.'

Yvette protested that she wasn't trying to win him, but when Janine poured the rhubarb wine she took it in and called softly to Alain to wake up. She smiled and offered him the glass.

He took it from her, his eyes smiling. 'I feel better now. I needed that sleep.' He sipped his wine and stretched luxuriously. 'I heard you girls busy in the kitchen. It smells wonderful. There's nothing so relaxing as the fire burning on the hearth and the women in the kitchen.'

Janine announced that the meal was ready, and they all sat down to table. All through lunch he and Janine kept up a steady conversation about the crops that year and what she planned for next.

Yvette felt quite left out, as she knew nothing about such things. As far as she could tell, Alain was quietly encouraging Janine to point out all the hardships of the life.

'You must marry again,' he told her. 'You need a man for such a place as this.'

After the meal, which they all enjoyed and did full justice to, they quickly cleared the dishes, the three of them working together. Then Janine retired to her bedroom to feed the baby and rest awhile.

'Daniel said he would come round later, about

four,' she told them. 'In the meantime, you two will wish to talk. Stay by the fire; the day has turned chilly and it's going to rain.' She closed her door behind her.

So Alain and Yvette sat before the fire like any married couple, she now in the rocking-chair, he in a carved armchair.

'She needs your help,' he said. 'I see no reason why you can't stay here.'

Yvette looked at him in astonishment. 'Do you really mean that?'

'You didn't let me finish,' Alain sat back in the chair, completely at ease, his toes stretching to-wards the warmth. 'You can stay here until your marriage.'

'My marriage?' Yvette's voice came out in a squeak. 'What marriage? I don't mean to marry.'

'You know as well as I do that the king and his ministers here will not accept that.' Alain was studying his hands. 'Another ship with little brides-to-be will be arriving in a few weeks, and you will then be able to take part in the Choosing—since you appear to have set your heart on that.'

Yvette opened her mouth to protest, but Alain went smoothly on. 'You've told me often I spoilt your chances by not permitting that before. Now you'll have the opportunity to make your choice in the same way as the others. Does that please you?' He smiled guilelessly.

Yvette felt trapped. She wanted to scream No, it didn't suit her at all, but why give him that satisfaction? She nodded dumbly, tears prickling her eyelids. If she couldn't have him, what difference whom she chose?

'I think it's always frightened you—that Choosing,' his voice was even. 'I'm not a cruel man; I'll help you. We shall have a little practice. Once you face a situation and try yourself in it, it becomes easier. Stand up, and we shall act it out.' He rose to his feet.

The reluctant Yvette did likewise.

'I shall stand here,' he went on, 'because the men are already gathered in the hall waiting for the girls to arrive. You stand over there by the door. That's right.' He nodded approvingly as the unwilling girl followed his directions. 'You've just come in from the bright afternoon or morning outside and you blink a little because the hall is dark, and shiver perhaps because it's colder in here. Now you advance and look at the men. No, no, not like that,' he rapped his knuckles against the table. 'A bold look like that will attract the wrong kind of man. Try glancing shyly from the corner of your eyes. That's better. You learn quickly.' His expression was kindly.

Yvette felt wooden, her face a mask to hide her feelings.

'Another step forward,' he directed, 'and one of them walks towards you.' Alain took a few steps so that he stood before her. He bowed. '*Bonjour, Mademoiselle*, my name is Alain. I see you're healthy, no broken arms or legs.'

Yvette made a face at him. 'You wouldn't know that about my leg.'

'Smile,' he directed. 'This Alain may be your future husband. If you grimace like that he may walk away.'

Yvette made an attempt at a smile.

'That will have to do, I suppose.' He put his hand on her arm. 'Yes, I think he'd reach out to you, touch you. He's afraid, too, perhaps as nervous as you. I can feel you shaking.'

Yvette tried to stop the trembling that his touch always roused in her. 'As frightened as I am,' she echoed. 'How could that be?' She was imagining herself into this future scene, yet she had the strangest feeling Alain was speaking for himself. Could that be? Her breath caught in her throat.

He nodded at her. 'Just as frightened—my name is Alain,' he repeated. 'I've resigned my commission in the army and taken the king's land as gift. That's where I was the other day when I didn't come to the hospital to see you walk alone. It's a big piece on the river. I shall settle there.'

'Is this the truth?' whispered Yvette, not quite ready to believe.

'Oh yes,' Alain held her hand in his. 'I'd hoped to marry a little lame girl with amber eyes—but she refused me—before I'd even asked her.' There was a glint of laughter in his dark eyes. 'I want a wife,' he spoke softly. 'One of the king's girls will have to do, since I can't have the girl I want.' His glance held hers.

'But you can,' gasped Yvette, realising at last that he was in earnest.

'No, she refused me.' Alain shook his head sadly. 'She said she'd rather live alone and be a dressmaker.'

Yvette stamped her foot. 'That was because I thought Monsieur Archambault meant to force you to marry me.'

Alain smiled. 'How could he force me to do what I wanted to do all along—almost from the beginning, I think—when I kissed you on the ship's deck I was astonished at how much I wanted you.'

'You were hateful to me!' Yvette found it hard to believe his words. 'You called me a foolish little virgin.'

'I was fighting myself as well as you,' he told her. 'And I had to keep on telling myself you were not for me. As a soldier I wouldn't have been allowed to marry you—but as a settler, ah, that's a different story. I have become a settler.'

Alain opened his arms to her and Yvette went into them. His lips held hers in a long sweet kiss. His arms tightened round her.

'Remember that day in the garden after you had given me the note about wanting to see me?' Alain raised his head and looked into her eyes.

Yvette nodded, too happy for words.

'I meant to ask you that day if you would wait until I had it all agreed,' Alain declared softly. 'But all you wanted to talk about was Liliane—and I was meant to frighten her—I couldn't bring myself to say anything after that. You had clearly come to regard yourself as one of my "men". You looked on me as you might your father. That was bitter news, but I had brought it on myself.'

'I never thought of myself as that,' Yvette protested, 'but you had made me feel I was too young, too inexperienced, too much of a nuisance . . .'

Alain stopped her words with another kiss.

Bliss engulfed Yvette. She abandoned herself to his enveloping embrace, her whole body tingling with the joy of his wanting her. Her lips opened under his, her tongue rushing hungrily into his mouth, her body moulding itself to his, clinging to him. Now she could give herself to him as woman to man with the passion not of a girl but of an adult. She had grown up and grown to love him as he wished to be loved.

Breathless, she drew away a little, still held in his arms. She remembered the past. 'My mother,' she exclaimed brokenly, 'your family . . .'

'What difference do families make?' he asked, his embrace tightening. 'This is a new country, a new way of life—freer than the old. You and I shall have a family of our own. That's the family who matters, not the ones gone before.'

'You know then about my mother?' she questioned, still uncertain.

'I've known all along,' was his steady answer. 'It doesn't matter. It's never mattered. I didn't hesitate because of that. Will you marry me, Yvette? I love you dearly. I want to spend my life with you.'

'Yes, yes please,' she replied, putting both hands to his face and drawing his lips towards hers again. 'It's what I've always wanted since that night you held me after. Marie-Rose died. Hold me tight again.'

They kissed, lost in heady promises and vows given and taken; this was the way it was meant to be. They had come together in love and longing.

The quarrelling was forgotten now, the misunderstandings forgiven.

The threatening storm broke outside with a thunder of rain on the roof and at the windows, but Yvette was held in the circle of his arms, safe and warm and loved. She had come through the ordeal of the Choosing. She had faced what she had feared for so long and, as he had said, it had become easier in the trying.

With her lips opening under his, her body vibrant against his, she was secure in the future of his promises.

She took a long breath and whispered, 'I love you, I love you, I always shall.'

His lips formed the words, '*Je t'adore*', as they claimed hers again.